TO DIE LIKE A SPY

Hurling himself forward in a rolling dive, the Kid went through the window in a cloud of shattering glass and framework. To the side of the window was a lean, vicious-looking halfbreed armed with a knife and already moving forward to use it.

Landing with catlike agility, the young Texan launched an attack of his own, swinging his knife around like a woodman chopping kindling. A scream broke from the man as the razor-edged blade tore across his body, laying through the flesh and into the vitals below.

"A:he!"

Belle could not guess whether it be words or a grunt caused by a strenuous effort. Few white people could have given her the answer, for those who heard that particular sound rarely lived to discuss it. It was the Comanche coup cry, "I claim it!"

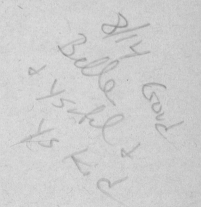

Bloody Border

J. T. EDSON

A DELL BOOK

Published by
Dell Publishing
a division of
Bantam Doubleday Dell Publishing Group, Inc.
666 Fifth Avenue
New York, New York 10103

ISBN: 0-440-21031-3

Printed in the United States of America

Published simultaneously in Canada

October 1991

10 9 8 7 6 5 4 3 2 1

For Daphne & Harry Chamberlain

1

HIT HIM WITH YOUR
PARASOL

"You sure you'll be all right, ma'am?" the sailor asked doubt-fully, looking around the deserted beach illuminated by the beacon fire that had guided them ashore.

"Yes, thank you," the girl replied, trying to sound more confident than she felt. "My friends will be close by. Carry out your orders."

With a Yankee steam sloop approaching through the darkness and the blockade-runner *Gabrielle* hove-to at the mouth of the bay, she did not dare delay the boat's return. Owned by British businessmen responsible for her presence on the deserted beach some miles south of the Mexican town of Matamoros, the *Gabrielle* carried a cargo badly needed by the Confederate States and must not fall into Union hands. So she stepped ashore and the men unloaded her two specially designed trunks. After setting the trunks by the fire, the men returned to the boat. For a moment they hesitated, but a brief flicker of light from the *Gabrielle* gave an urgent warning signal. Climbing back into the boat, the sailors set their oars working to turn it and make for the waiting ship.

Watching them disappear into the night, the girl could not hold down a small sigh. Tall, slender, although far from skinny, she had a strikingly beautiful face with strength of will and intelligence in its lines. Despite the hurried departure from the *Gabrielle,* and the fact that a blockade runner offered few facilities for passengers, her red hair looked remarkably neat and tidy. She wore a plain, stylish black two-piece suit, the jacket ending at waist level and hanging open over a dark blue shirtwaist. Apart from a single somewhat strangely shaped bracelet on her left wrist, she wore no jewelry. Striking an incongruous note under the circumstances, a dainty parasol was held in her right hand.

Even knowing of its presence, the girl could not make out the shape of the *Gabrielle* at the mouth of the bay. That did not surprise her, for the ship had been designed, built, and colored for the sole purpose of slipping unseen through the U.S. Navy's blockading squadrons outside southern ports. If Captain Horsfell acted as fast as she expected, within five minutes, ten at most, the boat would be back aboard and the *Gabrielle* moving away from the danger of the Yankee sloop.

With the ship went her last link to safety if anything should have happened to her escort. That possibility did not escape her, and grew stronger with the escort's nonappearance. While Mexico might be neutral in the War Between the States, it had troubles of its own. The French under Maximilian were fighting to hold the country against Benito Juarez's Mexican patriots. Either side in the brutal, bloody conflict might find the presence of her escort puzzling and know of a swift, effective way of solving mysteries. Nor would the French or Mexican forces look kindly on her arrival. From what she had heard, it might go badly with a lone young woman who fell into either side's hands in such a lonely area.

Hearing a slight sound, the girl turned to see what had caused it. Momentarily her spirits rose at the sight of the six men who came from the blackness beyond the fire, then dropped again as she realized that none of them could be her escort. Despite his name, Sergeant Sam Ysabel was no Mexican and all the approaching party could lay at least ostensible claim to belonging to that race.

All in all, the bunch approaching the girl struck her as being the most villainous collection of humanity she had ever seen. None wore a uniform, which proved little in the disorganized state of affairs across Mexico. Few of Juarez's supporters enlisted in an official army unit, and they fought in whatever clothes came their way. If the men before her belonged to a *guerillos* band, their appearances hinted at successful campaigning. Their clothing looked garish, too good, overdone in every respect—such as poor men wore when sudden wealth came their way. All carried handguns on their belts, ranging from single-shot, muzzle-loading pistols to an 1860 Army Colt. However, the knife each man wore at his waist would be his chief weapon. Tall, short, slim, or heavily built, one thing all had in common: their faces bore the stamp of evil, lust, and cruelty.

One possibility for their presence came to mind. Ysabel needed men to help his work. For all their unprepossessing appearance, the Mexicans might be working for him. Smuggling goods run through the blockade across the Rio Grande into Confederate hands did not call for the services of saints.

"Saludos, señora," greeted the short, wiry man in the lead, eyes roaming over her from head to foot in a lecherous, insolent manner.

"Buenas noches," she replied. "Are you the men who lit the fire?"

"There's nobody else here," grinned the small man.

Walking toward the speaker, the girl happened to glance at the ground by the fire. She saw a blackish patch, different in color from the sand around it. Raising her eyes, she saw the little man also staring at the discoloration. Then he looked at her with a wicked leer twisting his lips. Moving on, he came to a halt before the girl and his companions started to form a half circle around them.

"What you doing here, *señora*?" the small man asked.

"You don't know?" the girl asked quietly, standing with feet spread slightly apart and the parasol gripped at the handle and on the folded canopy.

"No, *señora*," came the mocking reply. "The *hombre* who lit the fire, he didn't have time to tell us."

"He didn't even have time to pray," another man went on.

Cold shock bit into the girl at the words. Taken with that patch of drying blood by the fire, they meant only one thing. Her escort was dead—and his position might be preferable to her own in the near future. Because of the danger of landing on a deserted Mexican beach, it had originally been arranged that the *Gabrielle* should remain offshore until her escort arrived. But the presence of the Yankee sloop had deprived her of that means of escape.

If frightened, the girl gave no sign of it. Nor did she allow it to take control and induce panic. Swiftly she reviewed the situation and made her plans to counter its menace. As far as she could see, only one course remained open to her. Yet she must time everything right if she hoped to succeed.

"What happened to him?" she asked in an even voice, as if she believed all was well.

"He died, *señorita*," the little man answered, giving her correct marital status for the first time. "That's his blood you're looking at."

One of the men, a huge hulk with a brute's face, pointed to the trunks and commented on them. Then he walked across and knelt by one of them, hands going to the straps buckled about it.

"What're you doing?" the girl snapped in fair Spanish, going toward the big man. "Take your hands off that."

"If he does, he can't open it, *señorita*," the little spokesman put in.

"Why should he open it?" the girl demanded, swinging to face the speaker.

"How else will we know what's inside?"

None of the other men moved. Watching them, the girl realized they were playing with her as a cat with a mouse. Sneering, lust-filled faces watched her every move, and she could guess that they hoped she would provide them with some sport. So much the better; her chances of escape were increased slightly by their attitude.

"Tell him to get away from that trunk!" she ordered.

"José's a bad boy, *señorita*," the little man replied. "Maybe you'd better tell him."

"And if he doesn't," another of the group continued with a grin, "hit him with your parasol."

"That will frighten him away," mocked a third.

Watching the big man, the girl walked in his direction. Although still crouching by the trunk, his body was tense to spring when she came within reaching distance. He hoped that she would struggle—it was always more fun when they fought unavailingly to escape from his brute strength.

"You watch her good, José!" warned the little man. "She's going to hit you with that parasol."

"I heard!" José rumbled, and started to thrust himself erect.

Considerable experience had turned José into something of an expert on the subject of rape, and he felt that he could guess at the girl's reactions. She would either stand still, paralyzed with fear, turn and flee, or make a feeble, futile attempt to fight him off. On previous occasions, given the chance, his victims did one or the other.

Only the girl did none of them.

Instead she advanced to meet him, approaching before he reached his feet. With a twist of her left hand, she separated the parasol's head from the handle and let the upper section fall. Doing so revealed a small steel ball around which her first two fingers curled. At their pull, the ball slid out of the handle on a short steel rod, which elongated into a powerful coil spring. No longer did she hold a harmless piece of feminine frippery; she gripped a deadly weapon.

Just how deadly she rapidly proved. Out flashed the parasol handle, driven by a snapping motion that imparted a savage whip to the spring. Taken aback by the girl's unexpected action, the burly man hesitated. Coming around, the steel ball caught him at the side of the jaw. Bone cracked audibly and José pitched sideways. Limp and unresisting as a poleaxed steer, the big body sprawled onto the sand.

After drawing the striking head of the spring-loaded black-jack from its place of concealment, the girl's left hand flew to her waistband. A tug at a strap freed the skirt, allowing it to fall away even as she struck the man. Taken with the sight of José going down, the girl's action shocked the remainder of the Mexicans into immobility. Rapacious eyes followed the skirt as it slid downward, to be met with disappointment. Instead of seeing what they hoped for, the men discovered that she wore riding breeches and boots under the skirt. While fitting tightly enough to emphasize the shape of her legs, the breeches lacked the attraction underwear and stockings would have offered.

Expecting to be met by friends, or at least supporters of the Confederate States, the girl had decided against strapping on her gunbelt and its Dance Brothers Navy revolver when dressing to leave the ship. She wished to avoid adding to the interest her departure from the *Gabrielle* at such a place aroused among its crew, and the gunbelt's contours would have been noticeable even beneath the skirt.

Although she regretted the omission, the girl wasted no time in brooding on it. Unsure just how much of a respite her unexpected actions might have gained, she intended to make the most of it.

Already the little man was recovering from his surprise. Springing forward, he shot out his right hand to catch hold of the girl's back hair. It felt stiff and unnatural to the touch; a fact that barely registered before he received a shock which drove all thoughts of it from his mind. He intended to jerk her backward, inflicting sufficient pain to make her drop the deadly thing that had felled José.

At the pull the whole head of hair came away in the man's hand. Expecting some resistance, he fell backward at the lack of it. Boyishly short black locks now replaced the full covering of red hair that had previously adorned the girl's head.

The sight added to the men's confusion and held them frozen. To their illiterate, superstitious minds what appeared to be a full scalp coming away at a touch—and without its owner exhibiting the slightest discomfort at the loss—seemed miraculous, even awe-inspiring.

"Get her!" screeched the little man.

At the sound of his voice the other men jolted from their daze, although, fortunately for the girl, not all at once. Snatching at the knife in his belt, one of the men flung himself into her path as she started a dash for the darkness. His other hand thrust forward to catch her right wrist as the blackjack licked his way. Instantly she whipped up her other arm, driving it at her captor's face. Her fist did not strike the man; in fact she appeared to deliberately keep it from doing so. Instead she raked the bracelet down the man's cheek. A screech broke from the man's lips as blood gushed from the gash that followed where the bracelet touched. Releasing her wrist and his knife, he stumbled away with hands going to the injured cheek.

Hoping to take advantage of his companion's efforts, yet another of the Mexicans flung himself forward. The girl pivoted around fast. With the smooth grace of a ballet dancer, she whipped up her left leg in a kick. Unable to stop himself, the man ran full into the rising boot. It smashed with considerable force against his jaw and sent him reeling aside. Only just in time did he avoid going headfirst into the fire.

It could not last, of course, and the girl knew it. Once the men threw off their state of surprise, they would quickly overpower her. Then—she did not want to think of that eventuality. So she must make for the darkness and hope for the best. One thing she swore: when she left the illuminated area of the fire, she would make them pay heavily and in advance for anything they might do if they caught her.

Lashing around with the parasol handle–blackjack, she caused a man to make a hurried spring rearward, and prepared to dart away. With a spitting snarl like a hound-scared cat, the man jerked the revolver from his belt to line it at the girl. At the same moment the smallest of the party slid out his knife and moved forward. There would, she knew, be no time to deal with both threats, even discounting whatever action the remainder of the gang might take.

A shot crashed from the darkness before the man could complete the cocking and firing of his revolver. Nor would he ever manage to do so. Lead ripped into his head, spinning him around and tumbling him lifeless to the ground.

Bursting from the darkness, two armed men dashed toward the fire. The taller—a powerfully built, black-haired man wearing a battered Confederate campaign hat, buckskin shirt and pants, and Indian moccasins—held a smoking Dragoon Colt in his right hand. A long-bladed knife hung sheathed at his waist. Although he seemed to be a wild, dangerous figure, the girl welcomed the sight at that moment.

Dressed in the same general manner, the second of the newcomers was tall and slim and looked very young. Bareheaded, with raven-black hair, he had Indian dark features that bore a savage expression. He reversed his companion's system of armament in that his walnut-handled Dragoon Colt rode butt-forward in its holster and he held the knife in his right hand. And such a knife! Two and a half inches wide, its eleven-and-a-half-inch blade sideswooped down at the end in a concave arc to form a needle-sharp point with the convex curve of the cutting edge. Firelight flickered on the knife, adding to the wild aspect of the youngster.

Swinging around, the small Mexican saw the younger figure rushing at him. From all appearances the youngster was allowing recklessness to override caution. Certainly the small man seemed to believe so. Out licked his knife in a low, driving thrust aimed to disembowel the rash intruder. Even as the girl thought to scream a warning, the youngster swerved in his tracks. The big knife moved, curving around to catch and deflect the blow launched by the Mexican. Then it drove forward. Shock momentarily twisted the little man's face, to be wiped away by pain. Razor-sharp steel sank into his belly and ripped across. As the knife slid free, blood and intestines gushed from the gaping wound it left.

Accustomed to sudden death though she had been forced to become, the girl could not hold down a gasp of horror at the sight. To her ears came the youngster's low-voiced grunt, but she could not understand what he said.

"A:he!" he barked, almost as if taking part in some barbaric sacrificial ritual. The word left him before his victim landed facedown by the fire.

There was no time to wonder what the word might mean, or give way to the nausea welling inside her. From the corner of her eye the girl saw a Mexican pulling out his pistol. Leaping forward, she whipped her blackjack in a backhand swing that drove its steel-ball head into his face. Teeth shattered and he reeled back with his mouth spraying blood. An instant later the big newcomer's Dragoon boomed and its .44 bullet struck the man in the left side of the chest. Such was the impact of Colonel Colt's hand cannon that the man hurtled backward when hit.

Out at sea something streaked, sparking redly into the air, and burst into a brilliant white glow of light that drifted downward again. Knowing it to be an illuminating rocket from the Yankee steam sloop, the girl felt a momentary alarm. Then she realized that it had been aimed to explode over the beach, which meant that the enemy ship had not become aware of the departing *Gabrielle*. Probably the sound of shooting had carried across the water and the sloop had sent up a rocket to expose whoever did it. Telescopes would be pointing toward the beach, possibly some of them powerful enough to make out the nature of the fracas. In which case, seeing three obvious *americanos del norte* fighting with a bunch of Mexicans, an investigation would surely be made. There were sufficient deserters from both sides in Mexico to arouse the interest of the Yankee captain, without his guessing the true nature of the trio, and to cause him to attempt their capture.

Clearly the Mexicans realized the danger, those in a position to do so. At the first warning glow of the exploding rocket, the two men still on their feet—one of them holding his bracelet-slashed cheek—turned and fled. Looking like a charging cougar, the youngster launched himself after them.

"Let 'em go, Lon!" barked the big man.

At the words the youngster skidded to a halt and turned. While the rocket's glow had died away, the fire still gave sufficient light for the girl to study her rescuers closely. Hard, tough as nails, but without the vicious, inhuman cruelty of the Mexican attackers was how the big man struck her, and she prided herself as a judge of human character. For all his shaggy black hair, buckskins, and generally unsoldierly appearance, she felt sure that she could identify him.

Then she looked at the second of her rescuers. All the savagery had left his face. Suddenly it took on a handsome cast of almost babyish innocence, apart from the reckless glint that remained in the red-hazel eyes. Young he undoubtedly was, yet she gained the impression that he had spent hard, wild years of growing that had left an indelible mark. Walking across to the man he had killed, the youngster bent down. Such had been his actions on arrival that, taken with his Indian-dark skin pigmentation, the girl thought he meant to scalp his victim. From what she had heard, although her personal experience did not support it, western men sometimes took scalps. However, the youngster did no more than clean the blade of his knife on the body's clothing, then dropped it back into the sheath at the left of his belt.

Before the reaction to her narrow escape, or to how the small Mexican had died, could strike the girl, the big man came up.

"Southrons, hear your country call you," he said, twirling the Dragoon's four-pound, one-ounce weight on his finger and dropping the big revolver butt forward in his holster.

Relief flooded over the girl and the fact that the man's words formed the opening line to General Albert Pike, C.S.A.'s stirringly patriotic version of Daniel B. Emmet's song "Dixie" did not entirely account for it. Maybe her rescuers looked as wild and reckless as the hairiest of the old mountain men, but the taller of them had given a password known only to a few.

"Up lest worse than death befall you," she replied. "You must be Se—."

"We'd best get goin', ma'am," the man interrupted. "There'll be a Yankee ship out thatways, I'd reckon."

"Yes."

"Figures. No blockade runner'd be sendin' up rockets that ways. Warn't there nobody here when you landed?"

"No. I thought that you would be when I saw the beacon."

"Right sorry about that, ma'am," the big man apologized, sensing the undercurrent of anger in her voice. "See, we'd just lit up when—"

"There's a boat coming, *ap',* " the youngster put in, nodding toward the bay.

Swinging around, the girl stared into the blackness but could make out no sign that he spoke the truth. However, the man appeared satisfied with the warning.

"We'd best get goin', ma'am," he said. "Grab a hold of that pannier, boy. I'll take the other one."

"Beach ahoy!" bawled a voice from the bay. "Stand fast there!"

"I'd as soon not," drawled the big man, striding toward the trunks.

A point the girl found herself in complete agreement with. However, she did not wish to abandon her property. So she darted to where her skirt lay and picked it up, then snatched the parasol's head from the sand. Just as she turned to follow the men, she remembered the wig.

"Don't like to keep on about a thing, ma'am," the youngster remarked in a conversational tone, "but that boat's comin' up faster'n a deacon headed for a new still. If we're going, now'd be a real good time to start, or sooner."

Glancing across the bay, the girl could see a shape darker than the surrounding blackness. Yet her wig lay where the little man dropped it, some distance from where she stood.

"Stand or we'll fire on you!" shouted the same voice, coming from the dark shape on the bay.

"Come on!" barked the big man, swinging one of the trunks on to his shoulder. "Let's get off afore he does it."

"Pappy's right, like always, ma'am!" the youngster stated, turning and darting to the second trunk.

Knowing that it weighed over a hundred pounds, the girl ran up and took the trunk's left-side handle.

"I'll help you carry it," she said, holding her skirt and parasol in the other hand.

Even if the youngster intended to argue, a shot from the approaching boat halted his words. The bullet passed between him and the girl as they lifted the trunk between them. Then they followed the big man, running through the circle of the firelight toward the protection of the darkness beyond. Another shot sounded and lead made an eerie "whap!" in the air by the girl's head. She felt the youngster forcing her to the left and realized that he wanted to put the fire between them and the Yankees.

Two more shots sparked muzzle blasts through the night, but where the bullets went was anybody's guess. Certainly neither came near the running trio, and a moment later they passed into the darkness.

From all appearances the girl's rescuers had made use of the bay and beach on previous occasions. Without hesitation the big man led the way to a level path that ran up the slope. Bushes closed in on either side once they left the smooth sand of the beach, and the path curved through them. Rising into the air, another rocket illuminated the area. However, the trio offered such a poor target among the bushes that the crew of the Yankee launch wasted no more bullets. Then the rocket burned out and darkness descended once more.

On drawing close to the head of the slope, the big man turned off the track. Followed by the other two, he moved a short way among the bushes and came to a halt.

"Just hunker down here, ma'am," he said, setting the trunk on the ground. "I don't figure the Yankees'll follow us too far."

Superbly fit though she might be, the girl was breathing heavily as she set down her side of the trunk. Looking back, she saw the thirty-six-foot-long launch run ashore and its crew, under the command of a midshipman, spring out. Armed with Sharps carbines, Navy Colts, and cutlasses, the nineteen men fanned out and moved toward the fire. One of them went up to the small Mexican's body and rolled it over. Jerking back as if struck, he turned and vomited on the sand.

Turning to speak to the men, the girl suddenly realized that only one of them was standing by her. The youngster who had helped carry her second trunk had disappeared.

2

THERE'S FIFTEEN THOUSAND DOLLARS IN THEM

"Where is he?" the girl gasped, swinging to the big man.

"Who, Lon?" he replied. "Gone back down there a ways to see what the Yankees make of it."

"But they might catch him!" she protested.

"It'd take more'n any bunch of webfooted Yankee scalybacks to do that, ma'am," drawled the man, with complete confidence. "He learned the game from the Comanche."

Satisfied, at least partially, the girl turned her attention back to the beach. Some of the sailors were examining the bodies, and two more had raised the girl's first victim to his feet and were supporting him. Another of the party handed something that the girl could not see to the midshipman. For a moment the young warrant officer stood looking at the object, the sailor between him and the watchers on the slope. Then he swung to stare up in their direction. The girl caught her breath, wondering if her younger rescuer had failed to justify his companion's confidence. Then the midshipman gave an order and his men returned to the boat carrying the injured man along with them.

"They're going," breathed the girl, watching the launch withdraw into the darkness.

"Figured they'd not stick around to look for us," replied the big man.

Landing on the Mexican coast in such a manner might be construed as an armed invasion, or at best be regarded as an intrusion against the other country's territorial rights. To be caught doing so by the authorities would bring about a bitter exchange of diplomatic letters, if nothing worse. So the sloop's captain had probably ordered his subordinate only to go beyond the beach if certain he could make a speedy capture. Seeing no chance of doing so, the midshipman wisely decided to return to his ship. While they took the Mexican along for questioning, the act could later be excused on the grounds that he needed medical attention.

For five minutes after the launch departed, the man and girl remained silent. Then he turned to face her, and she could see his teeth glinting white in a grin as he spoke.

"Now we've time, I'd best introduce myself, ma'am. Sergeant Sam Ysabel, Mosby's Raiders. Boy's my son, Loncey Dalton."

"I'm pleased to meet you, Sergeant," the girl answered, and spoke genuinely, not in the formal conventional reply. "My name is Boyd."

"Boyd!" said the youngster, materializing at her side as soundlessly as he had disappeared. "Belle Boyd—the Rebel Spy?"

Although the voice gave the girl a nasty fright, she restrained herself beyond the one startled gasp.

"I'm Belle Boyd," she conceded, a faint smile playing on her lips. "And they do call me the Rebel Spy, I've been told."

"This's surely a privilege and honor, ma'am," Ysabel stated, and his voice held a ring of truth. "Mind you, I should've figured who you be as soon as I saw the way you handled that scum down there."

"Lordy lord!" grinned his son. "I've never seed a feller so all-fired took back as when that short-growed *pelado** laid hands on your head and the hair all come off in it."

Respect and admiration showed in both her companions' voices. While she was pleased with it, the two men's attitude did not entirely surprise the girl. Through the war years, supporters of the South had much for which to praise and honor Belle Boyd's name.

Born of a rich southern family, Belle grew up in a slightly different manner than many of her contemporaries. While receiving instruction in the normal womanly virtues and subjects, her education extended beyond those bounds. Possibly to make up for being unable to have a son, her father taught her many boyish skills. Being something of a tomboy, Belle became an accomplished rider—astride as well as on the formal side saddle—skilled with pistol, shotgun, rifle, or sword and very competent at *savate,* the combined foot-and-fist boxing of the French Creoles.

Probably the skills would have been put aside and forgotten had it not been for the coming of the war. Shortly before the attack on Fort Sumter occurred, a drunken rabble of Union supporters raided the Boyd plantation. Before the family's "downtrodden and persecuted" slaves drove off the mob, Belle's father and mother lay dead and the girl was wounded outside the blazing mansion. Nursed back to health by the blacks, Belle learned of the declaration of war and sought for a way to take her part. Her parents' murder left a bitter hatred for Yankees that could not be healed by sitting passively at home —not that her home remained. So she eagerly accepted the invitation of her cousin, Rose Greenhow, to help organize a spy ring for the Confederate States.

At first there had been considerable opposition to southern ladies sullying their hands with such a dirty business as spying, but successes and the needs of the times gained their acceptance. While Rose concentrated on gathering information, Belle

* *Pelado:* A grave- or corpse-robber.

took a far more active part. Often in the early days she made long, hard rides through enemy territory to deliver messages and won the acclaim of old General Stonewall Jackson himself. More important missions followed, while Pinkerton and his U.S. Secret Service fumed, raged impotently and hunted Belle. Despite all efforts to capture her, Belle retained her liberty and struck shrewd, hard blows for the South.

Standing in the darkness, Belle tried to study the two men who had saved her life and would be working with her on the mission that lay ahead. She knew little about them except that the Gray Ghost, Colonel John Singleton Mosby, claimed them to be the best men available for her aides.

Sam Ysabel belonged to that hardy brotherhood of adventurers who pushed into Texas and helped open up that great state. Objecting to the taxes levied by distant Washington on the import of Mexican goods, he became a smuggler running contraband across the Rio Grande. Then war came and he joined Mosby's Raiders, to be returned to Texas for the purpose of resuming his old business when the Yankees took Brownsville. Many a cargo of goods brought in through the blockade and landed at Matamoros found its way to Texas, then on to the deep South, by Ysabel's efforts.

While none of the trio guessed it, young Loncey Dalton Ysabel was to achieve a legendary status equal to the Rebel Spy's in the years following the war.* Left motherless at birth, the boy grew up among the people of his maternal grandfather. His mother had been the daughter of Long Walker, war chief of the *Pehnane* Comanche and his French Creole *pairaivo,* head wife.

With Ysabel away on man's business, the boy was raised as a Comanche and taught all those things a *Pehnane* braveheart must know.† Under skilled tuition, he learned to ride any horse ever foaled, and get more out of it than could any white man. Ability with weapons, always a prime subject, took a prominent

* How this happened is told in the author's floating outfit stories.
† Told in *Comanche.*

part in his schooling. While good with his old Dragoon Colt, he relied mostly on his bowie knife for close-range work and called upon the services of a deadly accurate Mississippi rifle when dealing with distant enemies. In the use of both he could claim a mastery equal to the best in Mosby's Raiders. Few white men matched his ability in the matter of silent movement, locating hidden foes, or hiding undetected where such seemed an impossibility.

All in all the Ysabel Kid—as white folks knew him—would prove as great an asset to Belle's mission as he might have to a raiding party of the Wasps, Quick Stingers, Raiders, all three of which names had been given by Texans to the *Pehnane.*

Although interested in her companions and grateful to them for saving her from the Mexicans, Belle wondered why she found herself in the position of needing to be saved. However, knowing how little regard for discipline and orders such men usually possessed, she hesitated to ask a question that might mar their relationship. Almost as if reading her thoughts, Ysabel launched into an explanation.

"Right sorry about not being on hand when you landed, ma'am," he said. "We come down and got the fire started ready. Then Lon allowed he heard something, so me 'n' him went back to keep the hosses quiet. Didn't want no French patrol sneaking up and asking fool questions. We left Miguel, one of our boys, to tend to the fire. He warn't there when you landed?"

"Those men told me they killed him," Belle replied.

"The bastards—Sorry, ma'am. Only Mig'd been with us a fair time. They must've been slick to get up close enough without him hearing. Time we figured whoever the boy heard'd gone by, you'd landed and the fuss started."

"You came in time," Belle stated, satisfied with the explanation. Then she looked at the Kid. "What did the Yankee sailors make of it?"

"Figured us to be Mexican smugglers tangling with deserters, from what they said," he replied. "That wig of your'n sure got 'em puzzled, though."

"Damn that wig!" Belle snapped. "I knew I should never have left it."

"Too late for worryin' now, ma'am," Ysabel pointed out. "Go fetch the hosses up, boy. We'd best get goin'."

"But your friend—" Belle protested, looking back toward the darkness around the fire.

"He's dead, ma'am. Scum like that don't take prisoners— except maybe in a pretty gal's case and they kill her when they've done. Sooner we pull out, the happier I'll be. Those shots could've been heard by more'n the Yankees."

"Then we'll get going," Belle agreed, turning back to find that the Kid had made another of his silent, eerie departures.

Soon he returned, leading four horses. All were fine animals, but one of them more than the others caught the eye. A big, magnificent white stallion, it looked almost as wild and danger- ous as the youngster it followed; leading might be too strong a word in its case, for it walked free behind the Kid.

"Don't go near nor touch that white, Miss Boyd," warned Ysabel, following the direction of the girl's gaze. "My grulla's bad enough, but I do swear that damned white's part grizzly b'ar crossed with snapping turtle. Not that I need tell *you* any- thing about hosses."

"He looks that way," Belle smiled, accepting the tribute to her equestrian knowledge. "Which horse shall I take?"

"The bay. T'other's ole Mig's. We didn't bring but him along. Figured the less who knowed what brought us down here the better."

"I agree," the girl said, then a thought struck her. "But you don't know why I'm here, do you?"

"No, ma'am," Ysabel admitted. "We'll put those boxes of your'n on the packhoss and move out."

"Aren't you interested in why we're here?" she asked.

"Sure I am. Only I figure you can tell us just as easy while we're riding as do it here."

Loading Belle's trunks onto the horse took little time, as they had been designed to fit the official C.S.A. packsaddle used by the Ysabels. While the men attended to the loading, Belle approached and gained the confidence of the horse allocated to her. Although a powerful mount capable of speed and endurance, it would not be easy to handle. So she counted the time well spent. Swinging into the low-horned, double-girthed saddle—experience had taught her that the Texans rarely used the word *cinch*—she felt the horse move restlessly beneath her. However, long experience and a knack with animals enabled her to control her mount, then gain its confidence. As long as she did not commit any blunder of riding or management, she expected no trouble with the bay.

"Lead the way, Sergeant," she said, glancing to where her escorts were swinging astride their horses. "Head toward Matamoros and I'll tell you our assignment as we ride."

However, the chance did not come immediately. Deciding that they must put some distance between themselves and the bay, Ysabel urged his party on at a fast trot. Not until they had covered two miles and were riding along a path through heavily wooded country did he slow down.

"Nobody's following," he said. "Do you want to camp here for the night or push on, ma'am?"

"Push on," she replied. "I must go to see our consul in Matamoros as soon as I possibly can. Do you know his house?"

"Sure," Ysabel said. "And so do the Yankees. Unless you have to go there, I'd say stay long and far away."

"I have to report to him," Belle insisted. "He'll be in a mucksweat to know whether I've arrived or not."

"That figures," the Kid remarked.

"Not for my sake, I assure you," smiled the girl. "But for those trunks. There's fifteen thousand dollars in them."

"Is there that much money in the whole world, *ap'?*" asked the Kid.

"I'd say just a mite more," Ysabel replied. "You're taking one hell of a chance telling a couple of border roughnecks like us that, ma'am."

"Not if all Captain Fog told me about you is true, Sergeant."

"You know Captain Dusty Fog, ma'am?" Ysabel said.

"We've been on two missions together,"* she replied. "He spoke highly of the part you played in averting the Indian war those two Yankee soft-shells planned to start in Texas."†

"He's quite a feller, that Cap'n Fog," drawled the Kid. "I'd sure like to meet up with him."

Almost a year later the Kid found his chance to meet Captain Dustine Edward Marsden Fog,‡ rated one of the South's three top cavalry raiders and eventually gaining acclaim in other fighting fields.

Ysabel put off more discussion on the matter of Captain Dusty Fog. Satisfied that the girl trusted him, or she would never have given the information about the trunks' contents, he got straight down to business.

"That's a whole heap of money, ma'am," he said. "What's it for?"

"Have you heard of a General Klatwitter?" she asked.

"Is he one of our'n, or their'n?" the Kid inquired.

"Neither," Belle replied. "He's French. At least, he's nominally French. His command is made up of mercenaries from most of Continental Europe. He's at the town of Nava. Do you know it?"

"Sure," Ysabel confirmed. "It's in Coahuila Territory, maybe ten–fifteen miles in from the Rio Grande below Piedras Negras and Eagle Pass."

"That's correct. We have to reach him with the money as quickly as possible. Can you do it?"

"Five to eight days' ride, depending on you and the kind of trouble we run into on the way."

"The Yankee Secret Service don't know this yet," Belle objected.

"I wasn't figuring on them," Ysabel assured her. "We'll have to stay close to the river most of the way, and that's mighty rough country. The French and the Mexicans're apt to start

* Told in *The Colt and the Saber* and *The Rebel Spy*.
† Told in *The Devil Gun*.
‡ Told in *The Ysabel Kid*.

shooting first and ask who you are a long second. Then there're
deserters from both sides that've come across the river. They're
living as best they can and aren't choosy on where they get
their pickings. Top of them, there's the usual run of border
thieves, white and Mexican. No, ma'am. I count the Yankee
Secret Service least of our worries."

"We must get through," Belle told him.

"What'd be so all-fired important about a French general,
Miss Belle?" the Kid put in. "There's some'd say we've got
more'n enough of our own without worrying about the
French."

"Few of our generals can throw an extra thousand men into
the field right now," Belle pointed out.

"And this Klack-wicker *hombre* can?" asked Ysabel.

"So he claims. A full regiment of cavalry, armed, trained,
and loyal to whoever feeds and pays them," Belle replied. "And
with a battery of horse artillery to boot."

"That's a tolerable good bargain, all for fifteen thousand dollars," Ysabel commented. "Unless there's more to it."

"What's he fixin' to do, ma'am?" the Kid went on. "Come
down with us and help Rip Ford take Brownsville back from
the Yankees?"

"No. He will march west, cross the Rio Grande into New
Mexico, attack La Mesilla and continue north up the Sante Fe
trail."

"A thousand men can't take New Mexico," Ysabel objected.
"Ole General Sibley couldn't do it with at least twice that
many."

"And they was most of 'em *Texans*," his son continued.

"General Klatwitter won't try to *take* it. His objective is
merely to raid, do as much damage and grab what loot he can,
forcing the Yankees to divert troops badly needed elsewhere to
stop him."

"Why'd we need to pay a frog eater good money to do that,
ma'am?" the Kid demanded. "We could send some of our own
fellers."

"We don't have any men to spare," the girl replied simply.

"The war is going badly for us and every available man is needed right where he is. But the Yankees aren't in any better shape. Meeting a new attack will force them to withdraw troops from their field commands; they've no reserves worth mentioning."

"From Arkansas?" asked Ysabel.

"In the first place, probably," Belle agreed. "But that's one battlefront the Yankees daren't weaken to any great extent."

Which figured to anybody who understood the situation. Under General Ole Devil Hardin, the small Confederate Army of Arkansas held back a superior-numbered Yankee force on the banks of the Ouachita River. Given a significant reduction in his enemy's strength, he might even start to push them out of the Toothpick State. Should that happen, it would boost the flagging spirits of the Confederate States armies meeting defeat in the East and encourage them to stand firm.

"And if they can hang on in the East, even without pushing the Yankees back, it will have an effect," Belle went on after explaining the previous points. "Up north there's a growing feeling among the ordinary folks that the war should never have been started and ought to be ended speedily. They're seeing wounded brought back by the trainload, hearing almost daily of kin or friends killed. If their armies can be halted, with the appearance of the war dragging on, the civilian population will start bringing pressure on their government to make peace."

"Will *our* government have sense enough to take it, should the Yankees make it?" asked the Kid, in a voice which showed a complete lack of faith in governmental intelligence.

"If the terms are acceptable, which they will be, I can't see them refusing," Belle replied. "It's accept, or go down in defeat, L—K—"

"Could say either 'Lon' or 'Kid,' ma'am," the youngster grinned. "I get called both of 'em—or worse."

"Mostly worse and allus deserved," Ysabel growled. "You allow this here frog general'll do it, ma'am?"

"Of course. The fifteen thousand is only an advance payment, to be made if I am satisfied he can carry out his end of the bargain. I also have a bank draft for a further thirty-five thousand dollars, payable only after the successful completion of his share of the business."

"Now, I don't 'low to be smart, like the fellers who dreamed up this fancy twirl-me-round," drawled the big man. "So I was wonderin' what's to stop this here general just takin' the money, standing us ag'in a wall and shootin' us, then soldiering on for France. Fifteen thousand'd go a long ways, further when that's all he need do to get it."

"A series of letters and other proof will be placed in the hands of the French as soon as it becomes apparent that he doesn't mean to fulfill his part of the bargain," Belle answered. "The people who produced this scheme are playing for high stakes, Sergeant. They won't hesitate to do it."

"Would I be out of line in askin' who's behind it, Miss Belle?" the Kid said, guessing from her tone that the Confederate government had not formulated the scheme even if they approved of it.

"A group of British businessmen, mill owners growing desperate for cotton. They know that if the South loses, the cotton-growing industry will be wrecked for years and with it goes their source of income. It was they who contacted Klatwitter before he left Europe, made the plans, and provided the money to put it through. He received orders to sail before payment could be made. So the businessmen put the delivery of the payment in our government's hands and they passed it on to us."

"May *Ka-Dih* reward 'em for their kindness to a poor li'l quarter-Injun boy," drawled the Kid. "I allus did want to die young."

"*Ka-Dih's* the Comanche Great Spirit, Miss Boyd," Ysabel explained. "I sure hope he's watching over us. There's been some trouble, and the French put a curfew on in Matamoros. We'll not get through to the consul's house tonight."

"Then what do we do?" she asked.

"Stop with friends just outside town and move in tomorrow morning," Ysabel replied. "It's the only way."

3

FULL OF MEN WHO WANT
TO RAPE ME

Standing naked in the tiny attic room of a small inn on the outskirts of Matamoros, Belle Boyd allowed a giggling Mexican girl to apply an oily liquid to her back. Already Belle had used the liquid on her face, neck, arms, and other places accessible to her hands, turning the creamy whiteness of her skin to a brown equaling that of her assistant. With so much at stake, Belle could not take the chance of some unfortunate exposure revealing patches of white skin to arouse suspicion. So, explaining her needs to Sam Ysabel, she received the girl's assistance to coat the parts of her body beyond her reach.

"Is it all right, *señorita?*" asked the girl, putting down the depleted bottle of liquid and taking a mirror from the bed.

Carefully Belle studied the reflection of her back. Then she scrutinized every inch of her body, checking behind the ears, under her breasts, beneath her armpits, and between her legs. Not until certain that she bore no white flesh to betray her did she nod in satisfaction.

"It will do," she said in Spanish. *"Gracias."*

"You take much trouble to look like one of us, *señorita,*" the girl remarked. "Is it for a man?"

"Yes," Belle answered, deciding such an answer would be more acceptable than any other to her assistant.

"For Cabrito?" the girl asked sharply.

"No!" Belle replied hastily, knowing Cabrito to be the Kid's Mexican name. She recalled how the other had greeted the Kid on his arrival and wanted to avoid stirring up a feeling of jealousy. "He and his father are taking me to meet my—my sweetheart."

Clearly the explanation satisfied the girl and her air of hostility evaporated as quickly as it had come. Smiling warmly, she indicated the clothing on the bed and suggested that Belle dress herself.

While donning the clothing of a poor Mexican working girl, Belle thought of the previous night's events.

Although nobody had followed them, Ysabel had set a fast pace and kept clear of trails during the ride to Matamoros. In addition to a desire to avoid attracting attention, the girl felt the Texans might be motivated by a wish to learn her ability at riding a horse through rough country at night. In which case she believed that she had gained their approbation.

On drawing close to the town, Ysabel halted the party and sent the Kid forward to scout their way. Learning on his son's return that a French picket was watching the trail, Ysabel still stated his intention of pushing on to the inn. Once again Belle felt herself being put to a test, but believed that she came through it to the Texans' satisfaction. Moving on foot among the scattered bushes, keeping the horses as quiet as possible, they passed within a hundred feet of the picket and avoided being detected.

If the arrival of the Ysabels at the small inn was any indication, they were highly popular visitors. The owner greeted them warmly, accepting Belle's presence without question. Leading his guests toward his stables, he avoided the front entrance and made his way to the rear. There he raised a dirt-covered trap-

door and lit the way down an incline to a large cellar equipped
for housing horses. With the welfare of their mounts attended
to, the innkeeper helped the Texans carry Belle's trunks into
the main building. Such was Belle's confidence in her companions that she agreed without a moment's thought to their keeping the trunks in their room while she bedded down in the attic.

Over breakfast Belle and the Ysabels discussed their future
arrangements. First she must report to the Confederate States'
consul in the town, but she knew that doing so would be far
from easy. To appear in her present garb of shirtwaist and
riding breeches was, of course, out of the question. Nor could
she make use of a dress and wig from her trunks. If she knew
the Yankee Secret Service, and by that time she figured she did,
they were sure to maintain a watch on the consul's house. The
arrival of a strange white woman would be noted and steps
speedily taken to identify her. When it became obvious that she
had not arrived through the normal channels, conclusions—
maybe the correct one—would be drawn. Let the Yankees re-
ceive but one hint that the Rebel Spy had returned to Matamoros, and they would spare no effort to locate her. The mission
ahead stood to be sufficiently dangerous without needlessly
adding complications.

Fortunately Belle had come prepared for some such eventuality. A chemist working for her organization had produced a
body stain of exactly the right color to give her the appearance
of a Mexican: easy to apply, quick-drying and—he swore—
impervious to soaking in cold water, while hot water and a
special soap would remove it with one washing. That and clothing borrowed from the innkeeper's daughter gave Belle a suitable disguise.

Dressing did not take long, for the clothing of a peon girl
consisted of only a shift, blouse, skirt, and sandals. That meant,
Belle concluded as she glanced in the mirror on completion, she
could not carry the Dance concealed on her person. Nor would
her parasol, even reassembled, be less noticeable in her disguise.
So she would have to make do with the knife-bracelet. It would

not be out of place or conspicuous among the bangles of the cheap jewelry supplied to complete her attire.

"There is only your hair now, *señorita*," the Mexican girl said. "I have never see—"

"I don't suppose you have," Belle replied in English.

Her hair was kept cut so short for a purpose. In her trunk she carried six wigs—or had until the loss of the red one at the bay—designed by an expert and used to alter her appearance. To wear one of them so that it appeared almost completely natural, she had to keep her own hair cropped close to the skull. At first Belle felt self-conscious when not wearing a wig, but she grew used to it and no longer worried over other people's attitude toward her appearance.

Selecting a wig from the box brought up, Belle tried it on. She stood before the mirror, altering the long black tresses to conform with the style of the girl by her side. A knock sounded at the door as she completed the work. She crossed the room and opened it. The Kid stood outside. No longer did he wear his buckskins but was dressed in a torn white shirt, ragged white trousers, and sandals. A sombrero rode on his head, while a serape draped over his left shoulder. With his Indian-dark skin, he would pass as a peon provided he prevented anybody from looking too closely at his face. Those red-hazel eyes would give him away even if his features did not. Glancing at Belle, he opened his mouth to speak, closed it, and stared again.

"Miss Belle?" he croaked.

"Will I do?" she smiled.

"I'd say you'll get by," he enthused. "As long as you don't talk too much."

That, Belle knew, would give her away. While she spoke some Spanish, her accent could never get by. However, she did not intend speaking any more than necessary on the short journey to the house of the Confederate States' consul.

Seated alongside the Kid on the small donkey cart, Belle attracted no more than casual attention from the passersby. However, only a coating of vegetables lay on the tarpaulin that covered her trunks. Hidden among them lay her Dance and the

Kid's Dragoon Colt, while he carried the bowie knife concealed beneath his serape. Belle hoped that they would not find need for the weapons, but carried them in case of detection.

At first all went well. They passed through the narrow streets of the poorer section, entered an area of greater prosperity, and moved at a leisurely pace toward their objective.

"Won't be long now, Miss Belle," the Kid commented, sitting with the brim of his sombrero drawn down to shield his face. "Once we're through this business section, we'll soon be at the consul's house."

"I won't be sorry," Belle replied.

They continued along the street, passing the town's best hotel. Ahead of them, a burly French corporal halted. Studying the approaching cart, he stepped from the sidewalk and blocked their way.

"Hey you!" he said in bad Spanish. "Stop that cart!"

"Sí, señor," Belle answered mildly, jabbing her elbow into the Kid's ribs as a warning for him to control his temper.

"What've you got here?" the corporal demanded, walking forward and eyeing Belle from head to toe.

"Is only vegetables for the market, *señor* general," the girl replied, satisfied that her accent would pass unnoticed by the Frenchman. "My brother and I bring them to sell."

"Get down, both of you!" the corporal ordered.

Only a few people were using the street at that moment and none displayed too much interest in the scene. Such sights had become common in Mexico since the French began their occupation, and they discouraged undue curiosity in their affairs.

Once again Belle jabbed the Kid's ribs, and he dropped from the cart to face the soldier.

"Vegetables," the corporal sniffed. "Maybe there're guns under them."

"No, *señor!*" Belle gasped. "Just vegetables. What would simple peons like us want with guns?"

"You Mexicans are all the same—rebels," the corporal answered, glancing at her.

Then, without any warning, he lashed his hand across the

Kid's face. The attack came so suddenly that even the Kid's Indian-fast reactions could not avoid it. Caught with a powerful roundhouse backhand swing, he went sprawling to the ground. Luckily his knife remained hidden, but Belle knew he would not accept the blow without retaliation. Just let him clear his head, and the Kid would be up with knife in hand. Then either he or the Frenchman would die. Whichever way the affair went, her mission would be endangered. So she decided to lure the corporal away before the Kid recovered.

"Hijo de puta!" she screamed, catching up a tomato and hurling it.

Letting out a bellow as the tomato struck and burst in his face, the corporal sprang forward. His hands closed on air, for Belle had bounded from the cart and fled down the alley by the hotel. Determined to take his revenge, the corporal gave chase. He plunged around the rear of the cart, ignoring it completely, and ran after the girl. Immediately the pedestrians hurried away. Since their arrival in the country, French soldiers had plundered and committed acts of vandalism or rape unchecked by their officers. Any Mexican who interfered was likely to be shot on the spot as a rebel and troublecauser. So the few people who saw the incident played safe and got clear of its location.

Hoping that the Kid did not recover too quickly, Belle fled down the alley. On either side rose a high wall, at the end another street where she might meet more French troops, and behind her clumped the boots of the running soldier. Hoping to throw him off her trail, she darted through a gateway and found that she had entered a cul-de-sac. It was a small plaza, deserted at that moment, where residents of the hotel could take exercise or dine out of doors in private. What Belle found most interesting—and annoying—about the place was that it offered only two ways out: the gate by which she had entered a closed door leading into the hotel.

Even as the facts registered, Belle heard the heavy footsteps of the corporal drawing closer. She could not chance entering the hotel in search of an escape. Such a fancy place probably housed French army officers or officials, and any Mexican peon who entered—even for Belle's perfectly good reasons—would just as rapidly be evicted. Should she manage to raise an objection, the corporal would claim he was suspicious. A search of the cart would reveal the trunks. Belle could not see any French commandment turning away a chance to lay hands on fifteen thousand dollars in gold, even if acquiring it meant antagonizing the Confederate States government. Even if her story and identity should be accepted by the French, they might order her out of Mexico rather than become compromised with the United States. In any event, word was sure to reach the Yankee Secret Service and cause a search to be organized to locate her.

So Belle knew that she must handle the matter herself, dealing with the corporal in a way that would dissuade him from his intentions. Yet she must not kill or seriously injure him. To do either would start an investigation and hunt for the person responsible. Glancing around quickly, she saw nobody at the windows overlooking the plaza to witness what would happen. That made dealing with her pursuer easier.

Turning as she reached a side wall, Belle faced the man. A lecherous grin twisted his face as he advanced with arms reaching out to close on her.

"Damned if the country's not full of men who want to rape me," Belle mused. "I admire their taste, but not their style."

With the thought come and gone in a flash, she prepared to defend her honor. Just in time she recalled that she was not wearing her riding boots and that the sandals did not lend themselves to *savate* kicking.

Twisting aside, she tried to dart by the man. His right hand shot out, catching her arm and swinging her around. Doing so put him with his back to the wall. Taking her other arm in his free hand, he pulled her toward him. At first Belle approached with only feeble struggles and face twisted in an expression of panic, which lulled any suspicions he might feel at the easy capture. Measuring the distance, she whipped up her right knee at the exact moment when it would do most good. Steel-spring powerful muscles knotted to give force to the rising leg and the loose-fitting, calf-long peon's skirt did nothing to impede its movement. Coming with sickening impact, her knee struck between the man's spread-apart legs. Instantly his hands fell away from her arms. Agony knotted up his face as he stumbled back against the wall and started to double over.

Interlacing her fingers, Belle hooked the cupped hands under the corporal's chin and heaved. Lifted erect, he slammed into the wall hard and bounced from it. Nor had Belle finished. She wanted to make sure that the corporal could not raise an alarm for some time to come. Nobody from the hotel appeared to be aware of their presence in the plaza, so she might easily make her escape and reach the safety of the consul's house before he recovered.

With that in mind she caught the right shoulder of his jacket in her left hand, while the right closed on the open neck. At the same moment her right foot rose to ram into his midsection. As he bounced forward from being slammed against the wall, she shot her left leg between his open feet and sank rapidly to the ground. Her weight and the pull on his torso caused the corporal to tilt forward. When her rump landed on the hard-packed soil of the plaza, she thrust upward with her right leg. The corporal catapulted over, crashed down on his back, bounced once, and lay still.

Hoping that she had not done too much damage to her assailant, Belle rolled over and to her knees. Before trying to rise, she shot her hands to her head and adjusted the wig. Then she saw the hotel's side door open, and as she stood up, a man and woman emerged. They came to a halt, staring in surprise at the scene before them. Belle could imagine just how it looked, the corporal sprawled on his back and her standing disheveled by his head.

Neither of the newcomers had the skin pigmentation nor features of Mexicans, which could mean they were French. However, the man did not seem to be of Gallic origin either. Short, blocky, heavily built, he gave an impression of rubbery hardness rather than fat. His face had a jovial expression belied by the cold, calculating eyes. Clad in a Stetson hat, buckskin jacket, shirt, string tie, and trousers tucked into riding boots, with a gunbelt around his waist supporting an 1860 Army Colt in an open-topped holster at the right side and a sheathed Arkansas toothpick on the left, he looked like an American, but not the type to stay in Matamoros's best hotel. If it came to a point, he hardly seemed a suitable escort for the woman.

In height she would equal Belle, some two inches taller than her companion. Black hair framed a good-looking face somewhat marred by an air of superiority. She wore a mauve shirtwaist and a plain black skirt from beneath which showed high-heeled boots suitable for town wear or occasional riding. Full-busted, she trimmed down to a slim waist and out again for the hourglass figure currently fashionable. Studying her, Belle guessed she would be in her middle thirties. A fine-looking woman, yet hard and intelligent, were Belle's other conclusions.

None of which worried Belle overmuch at that moment. She realized that something must be done, and fast, to explain away the dramatic scene into which the couple were walking. If the woman was a French officer's or official's wife, she would not overlook what she saw.

Twisting her face into what she hoped would be suitable lines of fear, Belle lurched across the plaza. Collapsing to her knees before the woman, she began to babble out an incoherent version of what had happened. The effort taxed all her knowledge of Spanish, but she hoped that the man and woman would attribute mistakes in grammar or pronunciation to fright rather than the real cause. She also kept her face averted, in case she failed to adopt a sufficiently convincing expression to go with the hesitantly spluttering words. Then she received something of a shock herself. So much so that she darted a quick glance at the woman and studied her with extra interest.

"What's she talking about, Mr. Kraus?" asked the woman.

Not in French, but speaking English with a clipped New England accent and the tone of one who had received a good education.

Hearing the words almost made Belle forget her pose. However, she regained it quickly as the man replied. From his accent, he hailed out of Texas and he clearly understood Spanish better than his companion.

"She allows the soldier tried to lay hands on her, from what I can make out," he told the woman. "Gal's so spooked she don't talk too clear. Reckon she got scared and run in here. When he caught her, she pushed him off and he fell. Must've caught his nut one hell of a crack. Anyways, now she's worse scared that the soldiers'll come and shoot her. She wants you to talk up for her to your husband. Must allow you're some frog's missus."

Keeping up her scared babble, after the one brief pause, Belle continued to dart glances up at the woman. The guess at the age seemed close enough, for her skin showed the coarsening of time. Although she wore some good jewelry, a wedding ring was not included. Annoyance showed on the woman's face as she turned her eyes in Belle's direction. Just in time Belle dropped her head forward, not wishing to let a Yankee woman see too much of her features.

"Get her out of here!" the woman snapped in the tone of one used to giving orders. "We don't want to be mixed up in trouble between the French and Mexicans."

Clearly neither she nor the man felt any suspicion that Belle was lying. Bending down, she gently helped Belle to stand up. The girl kept her head bowed and allowed her shoulders to jerk as if sobbing.

"Come on, girl!" the man ordered in Spanish, taking her by the arm and turning her toward the gate. "Go back to your people. The lady'll not let them follow you. *Vamos, pronto!*"

Deciding not to push her luck further, the girl stumbled from the plaza. She heard the woman tell the man to give her a head start, which suited her too. Once through the gate, she discarded her terror-stricken pose and started to turn along the alley.

A shape loomed before her, bringing her to a halt. Raising her head, and ready to launch an immediate *savate* attack, she found herself faced by the Kid. Anger showed on his face, while the bowie knife in his hand told what had brought him off

the street. Then relief flickered across his features at the sight of
the girl. He opened his mouth to speak and Belle saw the danger. If the man and woman in the plaza heard a voice speaking
English, they were sure to investigate. Finding only two Mexican peons in the alley would arouse their suspicions. So Belle
took steps to avoid it.

"My brother!" she said loudly in Spanish. "It is all right. I
am not harmed. A great lady saved me."

Give the Kid full credit; he might be boiling with rage and
full of a desire for revenge, but he could still think. Darting a
glance at the gateway, he slid the knife back into its sheath
beneath the serape.

"Are you all right, ma'am?" he asked in English, but barely
higher than a whisper.

"Yes. Come on, let's get back to the cart. I've quietened him
down."

"For good?"

"I hope not. Let's move. There's no time to lose."

"Damn it, that lousy frog eater knocked me down!" the Kid
growled. "I'll just go—"

"To that cart!" Belle ordered. "Believe me, Lon. I've paid
him back in full for hitting you."

4

THERE'LL BE BLOOD SPILLED
AFORE WE'RE THROUGH

For a moment the Kid stood glaring toward the plaza. To the grandson of Long Walker and a *Pehnane tehnap'* * in his own right, it went hard to take a blow without repaying the striker in full. However, he studied the grim set of the girl's face and knew she would brook no arguments. Good sense helped him to reach the right decision. Turning, he walked with the girl to the waiting cart. Not until they sat behind the plodding donkey did he ask the questions seething inside him.

"What happened in there?"

"Like I said, I handled the corporal and he won't be bothering us for a spell," Belle replied, turning to look back along the street. Seeing no sign of the man and woman, she concluded they must have left the alley by its other entrance.

"Anybody see you do it?" asked the Kid.

"A man and woman."

* *Tehnap':* an experienced warrior.

"Mexicans?"

"No," Belle answered. "Americans. That's why I stopped you from talking to me in English back there."

"I figured there must be some reason," the Kid grinned. "Only damn me if I could see it. Who were they, Miss Belle— some of our folks?"

"No," she said definitely, then described the pair.

"Feller's Charlie Kraus, I'd say," the Kid drawled at the conclusion. "Woman don't come to mind, though."

"She did say 'Mr. Kraus', or some such name," Belle confirmed.

"That *posada's* not Charlie's sort of place," the Kid commented. "Fact being, I'm tolerable surprised they let him inside and I sure hope they didn't leave nothin' lying loose with him there."

"Who is he?" she asked.

"A border jumper, like pappy and me—only I'd not thank anybody to class us with him."

"What does he do?"

"Anything," the Kid replied laconically. "Kept out of the army when the war started. Fought Injuns and bad Mexicans for a spell, so I heard. Then he started running blockade stuff across the river into Texas."

"For the Confederacy?"

"For him and his partner, a skinny-gutted—sorry, ma'am— *hombre* called Joe Giss. They run in the luxury stuff that pays best."

Being operated mainly by private individuals interested in making a profit, the blockade-running ships carried more than essential goods for the Confederate States. Luxury items commanded a high price, so much so that the Confederate government laid down rules as to the proportion that might be brought in. However, some of the captains still ran complete nonessential cargoes, relying on unscrupulous men to dispose of them.

"I don't like the sound of this, Lon," Belle commented.

"Or me. Among other things, Giss and Kraus do dirty work

for the French and Mexicans both. If Charlie Kraus's around and gets to hear about that money, there'll be blood spilled afore we're through."

"We'll just have to stop him from getting to hear," Belle stated.

"He's got might handy ways of findin' things out," warned the Kid. "What do you make of the woman? Way you tell it, she's not his kind."

"I don't know. No wedding ring, which means she's not a wife from the Yankee consul's office. Unless she's cheating on her husband."

"Not with Charlie Kraus, or at that *posada*. Might be working for some Yankee shipowner though."

Belle admitted the possibility. Although New England stood high on the antislavery vote that had helped start the war, a number of its businessmen held shares in blockade-running ships and indirectly sold goods to the South. So the woman could be acting as a go-between for such people. The number of men called into the army caused many women to handle what had previously been male work, especially in the industrial northern states.

Seeing the consul's house ahead, Belle put all thoughts of the woman from her head. If she was no more than a go-between for blockade runners, it seemed unlikely that their paths would cross again.

Donated by a southern businessman, the consul's house was a fine, large building standing in its own grounds and surrounded by a high wall. Since assuming its new function, broken glass had been fixed to the top of the wall as a barrier against intruders. In addition, a Confederate infantry private stood guard at the front and rear entrances. Knowing that a vegetable cart would not be allowed in at the front under normal circumstances, Belle steered their vehicle around to the rear. As she approached the gate, the sentry moved forward to block her path.

"What's this?" he demanded.

"Vegetables for the consul, *señor*," Belle replied, not wanting to make her true identity known in so public a place. Across the street were other large houses in their own grounds and she would be willing to bet the U.S. Secret Service owned or rented one from which the consul's property could be kept under observation. However, the sentry showed no sign of moving.

"We've got all we want from our regular feller," he said, scowling suspiciously at the cart. *"Vamos!"*

"I think you should ask the corporal of the guard to come and see our vegetables, *señor,"* Belle answered, hoping the man would have sufficient intelligence to take the hint. When he did not, she continued, "Perhaps the corporal will not like it if you send us away."

Still the words failed to bring the desired result. Annoyance showed on the guard's face and he started to move forward in a menacing manner. "Damned if I don't take a chance on i—!"

Then he came to a halt as if running into an invisible wall. His bugged-out eyes seemed magnetized to the bowie knife that slid into view from beneath the Kid's serape and lined its needle-sharp point at the center button of his tunic. Held low and in a position that only the sentry might see it, the bowie knife gave added menace to the Comanche-mean lines of the Kid's face.

"Get the hell out of our way, foot shuffler," the youngster growled in a pure Texas voice, "afore I come down and whittle your head top to a point."

And he looked mean enough to try it, what with the incident outside the hotel and a complete lack of patience in face of stupidity.

Nor had the use of a cavalryman's derogatory term for an infantry soldier escaped the sentry's notice, adding to his sudden realization that the couple on the cart were far more than itinerant vegetable sellers. Having been employed as a guard at the consul for over a year, the soldier could guess what kind of people he was facing. Spies in disguise did not expect to have their identities revealed and possessed sufficient influence high up to make life uncomfortable for any mere private who crossed them. Maybe his present employment lacked the glamour of active service, but he preferred to remain at it rather than be returned to his regiment. So he stepped back and prepared to let the visitors enter.

"Act *just* as you would on an ordinary call like this!" Belle ordered, speaking English for the first time. "If you point out the kitchen, do it. Or take us there if that's what you normally do."

Should there be a Yankee watching, he must see everything done in a normal manner.

"Yes'm!" the sentry replied, but he had sense enough not to make the change in his demeanor too obvious. "I should shout up the corporal of the guard, ma'am."

"Then do it," Belle snapped. "We haven't all day."

"No, ma'am! Yes'm! Corporal of the guard! Back gate for the corporal of the guard!"

On his arrival, the corporal of the guard proved to have a better grasp of the situation than the sentry. Which did not surprise Belle, who remembered him from her last visit. In fact she knew that, despite the two stripes on his sleeves, Rule Shafto drew the pay and held the rank of captain in the Confederate States Army. Of slightly over medium height, he possessed the kind of average build and features that defy description. On occasion he could pose as Mexican, from hildalgo down to peon, a French soldier, or a border drifter as tough and coarse as any of that breed and escape detection.

"Vegetables for the consul, *Señor* Captain," Belle greeted in a low voice. "Hello, Rule."

"Pass them in, Tidd," Shafto ordered, without giving a sign of the surprise he must have felt.

"Yo!" answered the sentry, stepping aside.

"I had less trouble getting in last time," Belle smiled as the cart rolled through the gate.

"You looked different then," Shafto replied, for on the previous visit she had posed as the *amie* of a Confederate "general."

"Tidd's not the quickest thinker around. Comes in handy if we want the Yankees to know something. There's one of 'em buys him drinks regularly for what can be learned. Not that that's much. I make good and sure he sees nothing."

"How about seeing us?" Belle asked.

"I'll keep him away from the cantina until you've finished your assignment. What brings you back here, Belle?"

"A big one. You know Corporal Ysabel?"

"Sure. Hi, Lon. Where's your pappy?"

"Down to ole Ramon's *posada,*" the Kid replied.

"Act natural," Shafto warned. "The Yankees own that house back there and keep a feller in one of the top-floor rooms watching us all the time."

"That's bad!" Belle breathed. "I've two trunks in the cart that we have to take inside."

"Easy enough done," Shafto assured her. "We put up that cabin—for the guard—when we took over. The Yankees can't see behind it and we always unload stuff for the kitchen there."

Belle had already noticed the small cabin, obviously of later construction than the rest of the building, standing to one side. Instead of driving toward the rear doors, she directed the cart around the cabin and found that it concealed another entrance to the kitchen.

While members of the black domestic staff unloaded the cart, the Kid looked around him. Although he received information and instructions from Shafto, this was his first visit to the consul's house. The French knew about the blockade runners using Matamoros, but preferred that the Confederate States consul not take an active part in it. So all contact with the Ysabel's superiors took place well away from the house.

At the rear of the building lay a small open plaza and a truck garden. Along each side and, he presumed, to the front, were well-cared-for gardens with a number of thick, flowering bushes scattered around. Too many, to the Kid's way of thinking, for they offered places of concealment a skilled man might use. However, the high wall, with its topping of jagged glass, and the sentries at front and rear seemed to rule out the chances of anybody making use of the cover.

"Here you are, Lon," Belle said, holding out the Dragoon Colt. "Let's go inside and see the consul."

Already the trunks were being carried inside. Following them, Belle, the Kid, and Shafto passed through the kitchen and to the front hall. The servants set down the trunks by one of the doors leading from the hall, and Shafto went through it. Trying to tuck the Colt into his waistband, the Kid found its weight too much for the piece of rope that acted as a belt.

"Damn it!" he growled.

"Leave it on the trunks with mine," Belle suggested. "You're not likely to need it in here."

"Mr. Garfield won't keep you a couple of minutes, Belle," Shafto announced, returning from the room. "He has a visitor. Don't worry, he'll show him out through the library."

While waiting, Belle told Shafto of her run-in with the French corporal. When she mentioned the pair of Americans, he nodded his head.

"Her name's Corstin, Emily Corstin," Shafto said. "Cousin of Hayter, the Yankee consul, and down here on a visit. Or so I heard. Only that doesn't tell us why she'd be with a border rat like Charlie Kraus."

"I think Miss Corstin will bear watching," Belle remarked.

"So do I, now," Shafto agreed. "I'll see to that."

Soon after, the room's door opened and Winston Garfield, the consul, came out. A tall, well-built, elegantly dressed man, he covered ability under a mantle of amiable pomposity.

"My dear Miss Boyd," he greeted, looking her over from head to toe. "I'd never have recognized you-all. Come in, come in. I'm sorry for keeping you waiting, but that was the harbormaster come for his weekly payoff."

"You know why I'm here?" Belle asked, leading the way into the consul's comfortably furnished study.

"Of course," Garfield confirmed. "Have a seat, Miss Boyd. May I offer you a glass of wine?"

"I think I could use one," Belle smiled. "Have you met Corporal Ysabel?"

"Not officially," Garfield answered. "But I've seen the results of your work, young man."

"Thanks," the Kid replied, feeling just a touch uncomfortable in the luxurious surroundings. "Pappy said to tell you he'd bring down some more of that wine on the next trip."

"Hum! Yes!" Garfield sniffed. "And now to business. I trust everything has gone smoothly so far, Miss Boyd?"

"Well enough," she said. "We ran into a little difficulty on the way to the bay, but it all worked out."

While the others talked, the Kid looked around the room. Then his eyes went to the window, which overlooked the gardens on the left side of the building. The upper part of the sash had been lowered to allow a cooling breeze to circulate around the room, but that did not interest him. Even as he looked, he caught the brief flicker of a color alien to its surroundings in the garden. Constant alertness had been a lesson taught from early childhood, and the sight sent a warning ringing in his head.

"Is there anybody working in the garden?" he asked, cutting into the conversation without hesitation.

"Not on this side of the house," Shafto replied. "There never is when the harbormaster calls."

Before the reply was half completed, the Kid started across the room toward the window. He intended to raise the lower sash on his arrival and check that his eyes were not playing tricks, but saw there would be no time. That flicker of color had been no trick of light or imagination. A man was darting through the bushes away from the house.

Hurling himself forward in a rolling dive, the Kid went through the window in a cloud of shattering glass and framework. Behind him Garfield let out a startled squawk. Equally surprised, Belle and Shafto followed on the Kid's heels. They did not know why he was acting in such a manner, but figured he must have a mighty good reason.

While falling to the ground, the Kid found time to curse his luck in not having the old Dragoon available. The man running away from the window must be stopped and had a good head start to be run down in a footrace. Then another fact ripped into him. A flicker of dark blue had attracted his attention, but the fleeing men wore buckskins of a tawny color. That meant there must be two interlopers in the garden. Locating the second of them became a matter of vital importance to the Kid's continued well-being.

Not that the locating took much accomplishing. Catching a movement from the corner of his eye, the Kid swung his head to make a closer examination. To the side of the window, dark blue shirt and all, was the second man, a lean, vicious-looking halfbreed armed with a knife and already moving forward to use it. Holding his weapon Indian fashion, with the blade below the hand, the man launched a sideways stroke aimed at the Kid's neck. No white man could have avoided the attack, but the man struck at a part Comanche.

Landing with a catlike agility, the Kid dropped his right knee to the ground, thrusting his left leg behind him and lowering the left hand for added support. The other's knife almost brushed the black hair as it passed over the Kid's head. Then the young Texan launched an attack of his own. While thinking and acting like a *Pehnane tehnap'*, he gripped the bowie in the fashion of skilled white knife-fighter. With the blade rising ahead of his thumb and forefinger, he could thrust, cut, or chop with equal ease. He chose the latter, swinging the knife around like a woodman chopping fire kindling. A scream broke from the man as the razor-edged blade tore across his body. Designed by a man who had given much thought to perfecting it as a fighting weapon, the bowie knife possessed the deadly qualities of a cavalry saber. It ripped across the man's body, laying through the flesh and into the vitals below.

"A:he!"

Once again Belle heard the deep-throated sound break from the Kid's lips. Still she could not guess whether it be words or a grunt caused by a strenuous effort. Few white people could have given her the answer, for those who heard that particular sound rarely lived to discuss it. It was the Comanche coup cry,

"I claim it!" given when a brave achieved his ambition of killing an enemy by personal contact.

"Close the gates!" Shafto roared through the window.

Ignoring the stricken man, the Kid rose like a sprinter starting a footrace and went after the second man. Already the other had disappeared around the rear of the building. Mingled with Shafto's warning yell came a startled shout from the back entrance's sentry. Then a revolver barked, followed by the crack of a rifle. The kid heard a bullet strike the wall of the house and scream off in a ricochet, so guessed that the sentry had been hit and was firing wild.

Belle's hand flew to the top of her skirt as Shafto plunged out of the window. Then she realized that the garment did not possess means of speedy removal—which, in view of the skimpy nature of her sole piece of underclothing, was probably just as well. However, a peon girl's attire did not impede rapid movement, so she found little difficulty in leaping out after the man. Then she raced across the garden, following the departing Kid.

Bursting from the bushes, the young Texan looked across the truck garden to the rear entrance. The sentry lay on the ground, his smoking rifle at his side, but the Kid paid little attention to him. More important right then was the sight of the gate closing. Uncaring for the danger he might do, the Kid charged across the truck garden. He reached the gate and grabbed its handle, tugged, and let out a low curse. In passing on his arrival, he had seen a key in the gate's lock. It was no longer there. That lean cuss in the buckskins had been a man of some nerve, taking the time to extract the key and using it to increase his chances of escape.

Transferring the blood-smeared blade of the bowie knife to between his teeth, the Kid drew back a couple of paces from the gate. Then he sprang forward and leapt, his hands catching the top. Even as he began to haul himself up, Belle and Shafto appeared at one end of the building, while the sentry from the front gate came around the other corner.

"Look out, Lon!" Belle screamed. "Drop back!"

Brought from his post by Shafto's shout, the sentry came ready for trouble. When he saw the Kid climbing the gate, he drew an erroneous—if understandable—conclusion. Whipping the Enfield rifle to his shoulder, he took aim and prepared to bring down the absconding "Mexican." He heard the girl's yell, but realized he might be making a mistake just too late to halt the final rearward movement of the trigger.

At Belle's warning, the Kid released his hold and dropped back to the ground. Nor did he move a moment too soon. The Enfield's bullet kicked splinters from the top of the gate a scant couple of inches above his head. Spitting the bowie knife back into his hand as he landed, the Kid turned toward the girl.

"He's locked the gate on the outside," he explained.

"I'll go over and open it," Shafto answered. "See to Tidd, will you, Belle?"

"Of course," she replied, dropping to her knees at the soldier's side. "Did you see who the man was, Lon?"

"Not for sure," the Kid replied. "A tall, lean cuss in buckskins. But I know the *pelado* who was with him. It was one of Charlie Kraus's boys. Damn it! The feller who got away was Joe Giss most likely."

"Get some of the servants out here, sentry," Belle told the soldier who came up. "He's got a crease across his scalp, but nothing worse."

"Joe Giss allus was a lousy shot with a handgun," the Kid commented. "Reckons to be somethin' real special with a rifle, though." Then he looked around him. "Reckon somebody'd best start findin' out how they got in."

5

NOW THEY KNOW YOU'RE
HERE, BELLE

Following on the Ysabel Kid's heels, Belle Boyd watched a masterly display in the art of reading tracks. As he moved across the garden, the Kid pointed out small marks on the ground which she could barely see, much less attribute any significance to. He showed her where the two men had lain hidden among a thick clump of bushes before advancing cautiously toward the window and inadvertently attracting his attention. Then he retraced the route they had taken to reach their vantage point. Close to the wall he ducked under another bush and pulled out a strange-looking object. It appeared to be a saddle's seat without the horn, cantle, tree, or other fittings. A number of scratches and cuts in the leather of the inner side gave a clue to its purpose.

"They used it to climb the wall," Belle said. "Threw it on top to cover the glass and climbed over on it."

"Yep," agreed the Kid. "Come over afore daybreak and hid out."

"How did they plan to get out?"

"Same way, I guess, unless something went wrong."

"You mean they'd stay here all day until after dark?"

"Why, sure," the Kid answered. "Ole Joe Giss's long on patience and so was the 'breed. Happen nobody disturbed 'em, they'd lie up under the bushes and could watch everything that happened in this side of the house. They've done it afore. Not every day, but regular enough."

"That's going to please Winston Garfield!" Belle commented.

"As long as he don't lay too much blame on Rule Shafto," the Kid replied. "Rule's got more'n plenty on his hands one way and another. And he's from Virginia—they don't get trained right down there. Joe Giss learned watching and not being seen from Injuns."

"It's not for me to lay blame," Belle smiled, recognizing a hint of rebuke in her companion's voice.

Certainly Shafto did have plenty of work on his hands, controlling and operating in the Confederate spy ring based in Matamoros and organizing the blockade runners. So he might be excused for not having located the two men. Such a contingency would evade most people, although it was easy to be wise and raise points after the event.

"Why'd they risk coming up to the window?" the Kid said, half to himself. "It's not like Joe Giss to take chances."

"Probably they wanted to see who we were," Belle guessed. "Or to try to hear what was said. How long had they been there?"

"I dunno. Not long, but maybe long enough to hear Mr. Garfield say your name. He talks kinda loud and they'd be able to hear him."

"Yes," Belle agreed, realizing the implications of what the Kid told her. "Even if the man wasn't Giss, he must be working for the Yankees. No matter what Garfield told the French patrol, the two of them didn't come just to commit robbery."

Almost as soon as Shafto had climbed over the gate and unlocked it, a French lieutenant and half a dozen soldiers arrived to investigate the shooting. They belonged to a small force assigned to the task of policing the town and were clearly under orders to prevent open trouble between members of the Confederate and United States consular staffs. Stalling the French long enough for Belle and the Kid to hide in the house, Shafto then allowed them to enter the grounds and offered an explanation for the shooting which Garfield backed up. As the French authorities did not wish to antagonize either of the warring sides north of the border, the lieutenant made only a brief examination of the grounds and left apparently satisfied.

"Reckon he believed the story?" asked the Kid.

"He accepted it," Belle replied. "Can they trace the half-breed to Giss?"

"He's one of their regular bunch. Happen they try at it, they could tie him in with Giss 'n' Kraus."

"I doubt if they'll bother. But if that man did hear my name, we're in for trouble, Lon."

A view to which Shafto subscribed when he heard the Kid's findings. They gathered in Shafto's private quarters at the rear of the building and he listened to the other two before adding his quota.

Already there had been a noticeable increase in the Yankees' surveillance of the building. By the time he climbed the gate, Shafto could see no sign of the man who had escaped, which led him to believe that the other had entered the Yankee-owned house across the street. On hearing the man's report, the Yankees worked fast. Usually they maintained a watch from only one upstairs room of their houses at front and rear of the consul's property. When Shafto last checked, there had been four observers training telescopes from positions where they could cover almost all of the grounds and building. The increased scrutiny gave mute testimony that the man had heard Belle's name and that the Yankees regarded the Rebel Spy's arrival in Matamoros as being the prelude to trouble.

"They'll cling like leeches now they know you're here, Belle," Shafto warned.

"I know," she replied. "I think we could get by them and on our way in the dark, but they'd soon come looking. If only we could throw them off our trail—" She paused, then went on, "Suppose we make them believe that I've achieved the purpose of my visit?"

"How do you mean?" Shafto inquired, while the Kid sat and listened, ready to give any help he could.

"What's the most significant recent Yankee development, either here or in Brownsville?"

"There was a ship arrived yesterday across the river, with six of those thirty-foot steam launches as its deck cargo. And the *Waterbury,* a steam sloop, came in this morning."

In a trip down the Mississippi River aboard a submersible warship during her second mission with Dusty Fog, Belle had seen one of the U.S. Navy's thirty-foot steam launches. She also knew of them in connection with Lieutenant William B. Cushing's successful attack on the Confederate ironclad war-ram *Albermarle.* Small, fast, carrying up to ten men, armed with a spar torpedo and a 12-pounder boat howitzer, the steam launches proved effective craft in shallow waters.

"Those launches could mean the Yankees are planning stronger offensive action against the blockade runners," Belle remarked. "Catch them close in, when they're not expecting trouble. Two fully manned launches could deal with any blockade runner, even without using their torpedoes."

"Or they might be planning to raid up the Rio Grande," Shafto went on. "I've been expecting the Mississippi Squadron to try something like that down here ever since the Yankees took Brownsville."

"Either's possible," Belle admitted. "Launches would be ideal for running up the Rio Grande, raiding, and hunting for your supply trains, Lon."

"Yes, ma'am," agreed the Kid.

"Then they're what we need," the girl stated. "Let's see if we can make the Yankees believe I came down here to warn you about the launches and help in their destruction. That may throw them off the real trail."

"It might at that," Shafto answered. "And it's important enough for our folk to send *you.*"

Belle accepted the compliment without comment, although she could not help but compare it with the open or thinly hidden hostility that had often greeted her in the early days of the war.

"Can we bring it off?" she asked. "I mean, have we the means of doing it?"

"Sure we have," Shafto insisted. "I've been gathering equipment for a strike at the Yankee shipping in Brownsville harbor when the time was right."

"What kind of equipment?" Belle inquired, although she could guess.

"Torpedoes. I've a couple of keg floaters and one of the new drifting kind hid out down by the river. One of our raiders landed them at the bay where you came in, Belle, and Lon helped bring them here."

"How can you be sure the Yankees'll know you're in the game, Miss Belle?" the Kid put in. "It could be Cap'n Rule here, or ole Rip Ford from across the river doing it."

"They'll know I'm involved," Belle said quietly. "You see, they're going to capture me."

"You'd best tie that a li'l tighter for a half-smart li'l Texas boy like me to follow," the Kid drawled. "How's you getting captured by the Yankees gonna help *us*?"

"It won't," Belle smiled. "Unless I can escape once they've seen and recognized me. I've an idea that might work."

Listening to the girl's scheme, Shafto and the Kid decided that it might just work, given careful organization plus a little luck. It would be risky in the extreme, but the girl felt that the ends justified the means.

"How do we get a boat in close enough to do it?" asked the Kid. "I reckon the Yankees'll keep some sort of guard out."

"They have a guard boat working the mouth of the bay," Shafto supplied. "And the *Waterbury's* moored well out. Both her and the other ship will have some of the crew rowing guard. It won't be easy to get in close. I planned to send the torpedoes down with the current, let it carry them into the bay, and hope for the best."

"We must have something a bit more certain than that," Belle stated.

For almost a minute none of them spoke, each turning over the problem in silence. Then the Kid broke it.

"Didn't I see a big ole tarpon in the kitchen when I come through?"

"It could be," Shafto answered. "The staff either buy them or go out and catch them for the table."

"Best time to catch 'em's at night," the Kid said, almost to himself; then he looked at Shafto. "How well can you trust those folk of your'n?"

"They've had my life in their hands before now," the man replied. "And you and your father's, too, when they've carried messages from me to you."

The Kid nodded and grinned. "No offense. It's only that I've got a fool notion that just might work."

After hearing the Kid's suggestions, Belle and Shafto agreed that he had come up with a sound answer to the problem. Then Belle brought up the matter of the weapons they would be using in the attack.

As the adversary mainly concerned with defense, the Confederate States put "torpedoes" as a major item in their naval armory. The term covered what would later be known as mines, rather than missiles fired through the water. Showing great originality, the Confederate States Navy's Torpedo Bureau—established early in the war—produced many lethal devices ranging from simple bombs disguised as lumps of coal—which, smuggled aboard enemy vessels, exploded when fed into the engine-room furnaces—to complicated mines detonated in a variety of ways.

To her relief, Belle learned that the torpedoes in Shafto's store were of the uncomplicated variety. That would be of great help in the work ahead. So she went into further details, planning with care and trying to leave as little to chance as possible. Not until satisfied that all had been arranged and fully understood did she give the order for the other two to start. Neither questioned her right to command. In addition to risking her life by allowing the Yankees to capture her, she held the honorary —but no less official—rank of colonel in the C.S.A. Granted to her by the Confederate high command, the rank served when dealing with officious or conservative members of the armed forces who still clung to the belief that a woman's place was in the home.

The Kid left the house accompanied by Shafto and headed for the *posada* to inform his father of the latest developments. Once clear of the building, they separated—much to the annoyance of the Yankee who followed them—and Shafto went to make certain purchases from a store on the waterfront that catered mainly to the gringo trade.

There being no further point in trying to conceal her identity, Belle did not try. In fact the plan called for her to make sure the Yankees knew she was in the house. So she asked the servants to prepare a bath for her and went up to the room Garfield allocated to her. At her request he placed her in a room at the front and with windows facing the house from which one bunch of Yankees was keeping watch. The next move in her plan did not come easily to a girl of Belle's upbringing, but she went through with it just the same.

Entering the room, she crossed to the windows and stood where she might be seen yet give the impression that she was trying to avoid letting it happen. At that distance she could only make out a vague shape with the naked eye, but knew a telescope would reveal more. If the Yankees were doing their work properly, one of them ought to have spotted her by that time. So she turned and walked across to where her trunks stood at the end of the bed. Looking back, she could still see the windows of the other house and knew she would be just as visible through the telescopes of the Yankee observers.

"In which case, you're going to see a lot of me," she thought, opening one of the trunks to take out her shirt, riding breeches, boots, gunbelt, and other clothing. "I hope your eyeballs bulge out so far they stick in the telescopes."

After which sentiment, she stripped off the Mexican clothing, standing where the men across the street could see her through the window. With any amount of luck they were watching, maybe even passing word for their less fortunate colleagues to come and enjoy the view. When sure that she had given the watchers enough time, she slipped on a robe and sat down to wait until told her bath was ready. By all fair means, her presence at the consulate should be well established already. However, she must make certain and continue to let herself be seen around the house.

The Confederate chemist's claims about his skin dye proved to be true, for it came off in the bath and left Belle looking her usual self. Returning to her room, she repeated the process of cautiously letting herself be seen at the window, then returned to the end of the bed and dressed in her male clothing. If the Yankees across the street had seen her the first time, she dared bet they were watching in the hope of another view. Which meant they would notice the change in her skin's color and be even more certain that the Rebel Spy was back.

After an absence of almost two hours, Shafto returned with the required purchases. He delivered them to the girl and found that they met with her approval.

"Did you have any trouble?" she asked.

"Not much," Shafto answered. "We picked up a Yankee outside the house and he followed me when we split up. But I lost him before I went near the store to buy the clothes. He was lucky, that Yankee."

"Why?"

"If he'd gone after the Kid, I don't think he'd've come back. Those Ysabels play the game for keeps."

"I can imagine they would." Belle smiled grimly. "That boy scares me."

"That *boy* scares a whole heap of grown men along the border," Shafto told her. "I went down to the waterfront to see what's happening across the bay and have word sent to Colonel Ford, asking him not to make any moves against the Yankees tonight if he could avoid it."

Belle nodded in satisfied agreement. Despite his failure to locate the two men in the garden, she knew Shafto to be a shrewd, capable agent. Only the fact that he could not be spared from his work in Matamoros, and his absence would probably be noticed, had prevented him from being assigned the task of delivering the money to General Klatwitter. Many men in Shafto's position would have protested, maybe even have acted in a sulky, uncooperative manner, under the same circumstances. He not only gave the girl every aid, but showed himself capable of acting on his own behalf when a forgotten point arose.

Across the Rio Grande, Colonel "Rip" Ford commanded a small force trying to retake Brownsville from the Yankees. Trained in Indian warfare, Ford wore down the superior enemy strength by raids, alarms, and darting attacks. If he should launch one that night, the Yankee ships would be on the alert, far more so than might be the case otherwise.

"Will Colonel Ford cooperate?" she asked.

"He always has before," Shafto assured her. "The situation across the bay's still the same. Three of the launches have been lowered from the ship, but haven't left the harbor. Up to the time I left, only the *Waterbury* had put out its chain armor."

As a precaution against attacks by torpedo or war-ram, Yankee ships at harbor or lying off southern ports often hung a curtain of "chain armor" around their sides from about eight feet above the waterline and extending some twenty-four inches below the surface. Made of lengths of chain cable lashed together and suspended from a rod, the "armor" offered some protection and lessened the effect of a ram's charging impact or torpedo's explosion.

"The new drifting torpedo's designed to go under the armor," Shafto replied. "By the way, I've arranged for a good man to follow that Corstin woman when she comes back to the hotel."

"That's good," Belle said. "I've a feeling there's more to her being here than meets the eye."

They stood in the hall talking and then went on with their plan for confusing the Yankees. Returning to her room accompanied by a black maid, Belle changed into a dress. She handed the male clothing to the maid and asked, with gestures, for it to be washed. Sure that the Yankee watchers read her scrubbing motions correctly, and would see nothing wrong in a southern girl expecting a colored servant to wash clothes worn only for a short time, she followed the maid from the room. Then, to the maid's surprise, she canceled the order and took the clothes back again. However, being used to the eccentric ways of white fools, the maid asked no questions.

Shortly before dark the Kid returned, but he came neither in his usual clothing nor as a poor peon. Instead he arrived dressed in the style of a *vaquero* and riding his huge stallion, which had turned into a piebald. Clothed in such a manner, he could wear his normal weapons. So the Dragoon Colt hung in its holster, the bowie knife rode its sheath, and his Mississippi rifle was in the saddleboot.

"It's an old trick," he explained, seeing the girl studying the black patches on the stallion's white coat. "Some powder a *Pehnane tsukup*, old man, makes up for us. It stands up to a fair washing in river or rain."

"I don't think anybody across there will recognize you," Belle replied, curiosity satisfied. "Are you ready?"

"Why, sure," the Kid answered. "Pappy'll be waiting for you when we're all through. With luck, we'll win you a day's head start afore they know you've gone."

6

HELL'S FIRE. IT'S A WOMAN

Rising to the surface, a tarpon over five feet long sent a swirling eddy in the direction of the Yankee guard boat and submerged again. By that time such appearances had become so common that the sailors rowing guard across the mouth of Brownsville's harbor no longer commented when one occurred. At that early hour of the evening, hardly past eight o'clock, they acted in a far more lax manner than later in the night, or on another station. Further north along the coast, attacks by Confederate submersibles, war-rams, or other surface vessels kept the blockading fleets constantly on the alert. No such alarms had come in Brownsville, Colonel Rip Ford being a plainsman, skilled at land fighting but with no knowledge, or means, of making war on water.

However, the relaxed performance of duty did not cause the men to overlook the two boats out on the river. One halted some way upstream, hanging in the current, while the other dropped down closer to the guard boat's line of patrol.

"Ahoy, there!" the midshipman commanding the guard boat called. "What boat's that, then?"

At the same moment he nodded and a man uncovered the head of a bull's-eye lantern to illuminate the other boat. Two black men lowered heavy weights on ropes to halt the boat's progress and a third held a powerful fishing pole. Turning toward the speaker, the third black answered.

"We'ns out fishin' fo' tahp'n, sah," he said, holding up his line with a small bait fish kicking on the hook. "They am runnin' just now."

Seeing the man in his ragged shirt and pants, nobody would recognize him as the immaculate butler from the Confederate consulate. To the midshipman, raised in New England, the trio in the boat looked like any other ragged, ordinary blacks to be seen south of the Mason-Dixon line.

"Guard boat ahoy!" bellowed a voice from the steam sloop moored just inside the harbor entrance. "What's that boat doing?"

"It's just some coons fishing, sir," the midshipman called back. "Want for me to move 'em on?"

"No, they're doing no harm. If they catch one, have it sent aboard here."

"Aye, aye, sir."

"Could you-all put out dat light, sah?" the butler asked. "It am scarin' the tahp'n an' Ah surely don' want Cousin Rastus along there to catch one if Ah don't. When dat happens, his missus takes on and boasts about it and dat gives mah woman the miseries and Ah don' get a lick o' peace."

"We wouldn't want that," grinned the midshipman and gave the required order.

Light or no light, the tarpon did not appear to be frightened away and it seemed that Cousin Rastus's wife would have nothing to boast about the following day. Dropping in his bait as the light went out, the butler allowed it to float down the river. Barely had it gone three yards when there came a vicious swirl in the water and the fishing pole bowed over violently. Then a tarpon shot into the air, rising in the kind of leap fast gaining its kind the reputation of being superb sporting fish. Again the tarpon jumped, arching its body high as it tried to throw the hooks embedded in its jaws.

Just about to give the order to resume their patrol, the midshipman closed his mouth. Sitting back, he watched the spectacular fight, pleased with the break in the monotonous routine.

Treading water in an effort to stem back against the current, Belle Boyd heard the commotion and guessed what had happened. It seemed that the fates looked kindly on her enterprise. At best she hoped that the blacks would be allowed to carry on fishing, but expected them to be ordered away. Having a tarpon take the bait was a choice, unexpected piece of luck.

Luck or not, she refused to relax and become complacent. Across the bay, Shafto ought to be releasing his keg torpedo toward the second ship by that time. She must wait until sure before turning free the piece of driftwood from which her own device hung suspended below the surface.

Of the two, Belle was handling the more dangerous assignment. True, Shafto had swum into the harbor, but sufficient tarpon had shown inside for him to pass unnoticed, or unsuspected. His torpedo consisted of a waterproofed wooden keg containing one hundred pounds of gunpowder, with conical pine ends giving a streamlined shape easy to handle in the water, weighted down to the desired level. As long as he avoided knocking the five percussion detonators on the sides and top of the keg, he ran little risk from the torpedo.

Designed to counter chain armor, the device hanging so close to Belle was a more tricky thing entirely. Its firing charge, in a metal cylinder 16½ inches long and with a diameter of 11½ inches, might be less than the keg's, but the firing mechanism was more complicated. Attached to the bottom of the cylinder, a propeller operated gears which released a spring-loaded plunger to fire the charge. As long as the propellers pointed forward, the torpedo remained inoperative. When its driftwood support swept against the target, the dangling torpedo swung under the armor, turned, and set the mechanism into operation.

A good idea, directing the charge where it would do most

damage and explode at the right time. However—and here lay the snag—if for any reason the propeller case turned early, there would be a premature explosion.

Slowly she drifted closer to the steam sloop, seeing its bulk looming up ahead. Then she decided that the time had come.

Using the device by which the two men had entered the consulate grounds, Belle, the Kid, and Shafto had left unseen by the Yankee observers. They passed through the town to where the blacks and Shafto's man waited with the boats. Already the torpedoes lay aboard "Cousin Rastus"'s boat, and they moved into position. With the greater distance to cover, Shafto left first and Belle followed when sure he would be almost in place. The tidal current ran at a good speed, sweeping into the bay in a manner calculated to carry home the torpedoes. Everything went according to plan, without any hitch to delay or endanger its effective working.

Belle released the driftwood, watching it lurch forward and holding down a gulp of concern. No explosion came, so all must still be well beneath the surface. Turning, she started to swim away in the opposite direction and toward the guard boat. At first she went carefully, using a breast stroke and keeping her feet beneath the surface to minimize the noise she made. However, on drawing close to the boat, she struck out and splashed with her arms.

"What's that?" one of the boat's crew asked, turning his head her way.

"Another tarpon," replied his companion on the thwart.

For a moment Belle thought that the men would dismiss her as another of the big fish. However, the midshipman looked her way and came to his feet.

"Tarpon, hell!" he exclaimed. "It's a swimmer. After him, men!"

Powerful arms worked the oars, sending the boat leaping in Belle's direction. She continued to swim, giving the impression that she was seeking to escape. Surging up, the boat ranged alongside her and hands reached down to catch her by the arm.

"Come on, mate," said a voice. "Don't struggle or I'll have

to crack your skull. You shouldn't've tried to run, you'd never reach the other side."

Just as Belle hoped, the men thought of her as a deserter from one of the ships. She intended to alter that as soon as possible. Another set of arms came down to catch her free wrist. Then the two sailors started to haul her upward. Bracing her feet against the side of the boat, she struggled against the pull. With a growl of annoyance, the man on her left released her wrist with one hand and grabbed at the front of her shirt. She felt his hand close, loosen, feel at her breast, then jerk away.

"Hell's fire. It's a woman!" the sailor gasped.

"Get your stinking Yankee hands off of me!" Belle screamed, sounding as feminine as she could manage.

Excitement welled up among the boat's crew, and all thought of the fight between the butler and tarpon were forgotten. Then the midshipman's voice cut through the undisciplined row.

"Belay that bilge!" he barked, and waited until silence fell on the crew. "Put a light on her, Torrey. Let's see what the hell we've landed."

"Landed" might be too premature a term, for the two sailors had not yet hauled Belle into the boat. The discovery that their captive was a woman handed them enough of a shock that they just sat holding her instead of raising her over the gunwale. Hanging in their hands, both bare feet firmly pressed against the side of the boat, Belle prepared to hand her captors another shock. She felt a slight upward strain and knew the men had partially recovered from the surprise of their original discovery —and the explosions of the torpedoes still had not come to give the diversion she needed.

"You'll make ensign at least for this, brassbounder," she told the midshipman in a voice throbbing with well-assumed venom. "You've just captured Belle Boyd."

Once again the pull upward ended and the sailors stared at her.

"The Rebel Spy!" a man announced in an excited voice.

Then he and all but Belle's captors of the crew started to
stand up, wishing to take a look at the legendary figure.

Despite all his attempts, Pinkerton, then head of the United
States Secret Service, had failed to prevent news of Belle Boyd's
activities from appearing in the Yankee press. So her fame had
spread and there could be few members of the federal armed
forces who had not heard of the Rebel Spy. Aware of that fact,
Belle used it to buy her a little more time. Once in the boat,
escape would be far harder than while still outside.

Even as the sailor with the lantern uncovered its face and
directed a beam of light on Belle, showing without any doubt—
due to the way the soaking shirt clung to her torso—that she
was a woman, the required diversion came.

Carried against the side of the *Waterbury*, the piece of driftwood hung against the chain armor. Not so the torpedo that
dangled at the end of a six-foot triangle of rope fastened to the
driftwood. Continuing forward, the torpedo passed beneath the
hem of the armor and, as the rope drew tight, lifted until
the pressure of the water forced it against the bottom of the
sloop. Having achieved its purpose in circumventing the chain
armor, the torpedo needed only to complete its work. The current beneath the sloop acted on the torpedo's propellors, causing them to turn, operating the gearing that released the
coilspring. Up slammed the plunger, hurled by the released
spring, to strike the detonator. With a dull roar, the powder
charge ignited. A gaping hole ripped in the *Waterbury's* bottom,
allowing the muddy water of the Rio Grande to gush in.

Nor did the effect end there. Still suspended on the side of
the guard boat, Belle felt the concussion-spread wave arrive.
Unlike the sailors, she expected—or hoped for—the explosion
and was ready to take advantage of it. Given time, the guard
boat's crew might have realized why the Rebel Spy had been
found so close to a Yankee warship and raised the alarm, but
that time was not granted to them. Taken completely by surprise, two of the standing men went over the side as the boat
rose and pitched on the wave. The lantern flew from its holder's
hand, struck the gunwale, and flopped into the river.

No less startled than their companions, the two men holding Belle relaxed their grip. Ready for that to happen, the girl thrust herself backward. Using all the strength in her powerful legs, she tore free from her captors' surprise-loosened hands. She went away from the boat, twisting around and diving beneath the surface of the water. Then she started to swim upstream in search of her companions.

At the same moment that Belle jerked herself free from the sailors, the second torpedo made its presence felt. Caught by the spreading wave from the *Waterbury,* the keg torpedo crashed into the side of the second ship. Crushed against the side, two of the torpedo's percussion detonators sparked their fire into the waiting charge. One hundred pounds of gunpowder exploded with a roar that far exceeded the water-deadened boom of the drifting torpedo's detonation. For some reason the ship's captain had not ordered his chain armor to be spread, so the torpedo exploded against the bare side and blasted open a large hole.

Only by an effort of balance and skilled handling did the midshipman and crew prevent the guard boat from capsizing. Horrible oaths ripped the air and gurgling yells rose from the two men in the water. Then the midshipman realized that his prize captive had escaped. Standing up, he glared around him. He saw that the blacks' fishing boat was rowing hurriedly away from them, which did not surprise him. No black would wish to become involved in the fighting between rebels and Yankees. However, there was no sign of the girl.

"Torrey!" he yelled. "Where's that God-damned lantern?"

"Over the son-of-a-bitching side!" the sailor answered.

Although Torrey would never know it, the loss of the lantern probably saved his life. Upstream, in "Cousin Rastus" 's boat, the Ysabel Kid stood holding his Mississippi rifle ready to shoot anybody who used a light in an attempt to locate the swimming girl.

However, the attempt could not be made. Nor did the guard boat's crew try to find Belle by rowing upstream. Rockets rose into the air from both ships, flares glowed to illuminate the harbor, rattles and drumrolls sounded the alarm. In the flickering glare of artificial light, the midshipman saw that his boat's crew would be needed more urgently than in making a search for their escaped prisoner, even though she claimed to be the Rebel Spy.

Taking in water fast through the gaping hole ripped in her bottom, the *Waterbury* would need every hand at the pumps or for other work if she was to be saved. Nor did the second ship look to be in any better shape, holed at the waterline and already beginning to list. Desperately concerned with trying to keep their vessels afloat, nobody gave a thought to the second boat even though one of the rockets revealed it held two blacks and two white men. Before the rocket's glow died away, Rule Shafto reached the boat and hauled himself aboard.

"Belle—?" he asked.

"Coming now," the Kid replied, pointing.

A tired Belle reached the boat and once again felt hands taking hold of her. Only this time she knew them to be friendly and did not struggle against their pull. Up she rose, over the boat's gunwale, and flopped exhausted on a thwart.

"You all right, Miss Belle?" the Kid asked anxiously, draping a blanket around her.

"Ye—Yes," she replied. "Ru—Rule—?"

"Here," Shafto answered, sounding just as exhausted. "Get going, boys."

Without needing urging, the blacks started to row the boat at angle upstream and toward the Mexican shore. Already the explosions and confusion in the Brownsville harbor were attracting attention. However, the French did not maintain any naval force in Matamoros harbor, so any danger would come from their army patrols.

"Maybe the Yankees'll cut loose with their cannons," the Kid remarked as he and Shafto's white assistant took up two more oars.

"That's not likely," Belle replied. "If they miss, the ball will probably ricochet into Matamoros. They won't risk that."

"I'd say they've got their hands full right now, without bothering about us," Shafto went on. "Make straight for the hide-out, boys."

"We've got clean away," the Kid breathed as the boat pulled alongside a wooden pier.

"Maybe," Shafto answered. "There's still the French curfew and Yankee Secret Service to beat. George, you'd best stay down here for the night."

"Yes, sah, Massa Rule," replied one of the black oarsmen. "We'll do that."

"How about Amos and his men?" Belle inquired, meaning the butler.

"They'll lay up until morning and then come ashore," Shafto explained. "If possible we want to avoid their being tied in with this raid."

Belle could understand the reason for the precaution. If the Yankees could prove Garfield knew of the raid, he would be discredited. Even if the French allowed the Confederate consulate to continue, it would be so closely watched that its use as a base for further operations would become negligible.

They landed unseen, leaving the boat at its moorings and with nothing to show they had used it. Then they went to the place from which the expedition had been launched. Ostensibly a warehouse owned by a British trading company, the building served as a base for shipping Texas-grown cotton and other produce, or storing goods run through the blockade until the Ysabels could arrange for their delivery across the Rio Grande.

Leaving the blacks with the white man, Belle, the Kid, and Shafto pushed on through the town's curfew-emptied streets. Guided and aided by the Kid's cat-keen eyes and remarkably keen ears, the trio avoided contact with the French patrols enforcing the curfew. The wisdom of taking an indirect route to the consulate showed on their arrival. Reaching the rear of the grounds, they found the Yankee watchers gone from the street, probably to investigate the disturbance at the river. So they entered the grounds through the rear gate without being detected.

Once inside, however, Belle went ahead with her plan of

allowing the Yankees to know that she had taken an active part in the raid. Before going upstairs, she had water tipped over her. Then, in her room, she lit the lantern and felt sure her soaked condition would be noticed. If so, the watchers ought to take the point that she had recently been in the water.

Standing at the foot of the bed, where she knew the men across the street could see her, she steeled herself for a further disrobing. After peeling off the wet garments, she took up a towel and began to dry herself. With that completed, she started to dress in the clothing bought for her by Shafto. Pulling the black shirt and trousers on over a change of underwear, she looked around the room. Everything was as she left it. Her trunks stood open, clothing inside. However, the money and a few vital items had been unloaded before the trunks came up and were waiting for her down below, packed in a set of saddlebags.

Then, acting as if on an afterthought, she crossed to the window and started to draw down the hanging drapes, but not to the bottom. While the men across the street could still see into the room, their view had been curtailed. For one thing they could no longer see higher than slightly above the girl's waist as she walked about, although they were still able to see the bed.

Leaving the room, she found the Kid waiting in the hall. He also wore a black shirt and pants, they being the only matching garments Shafto could find of suitable sizes. Belle thought the color distinctive enough for their purpose.

"Reckon I'll get by?" he asked, with a glance at the room's door.

"I think I've a better shape," Belle replied with a smile. "But with the curtains drawn down, it's likely the Yankees won't notice the difference. You'd best not walk around too much, though."

"That's for sure," he answered, also grinning. "I'll give you 'n' pappy a day's head start, more if the Yankees look to be fooled."

"And then?"

"I'll come after you."

"Will you be able to find us?"

"I'm *Nemenuh,* of The People, the Comanche," the Kid told her with quiet, reassuring dignity. "I'll find you."

"But two days, or even one day's, start—" Belle went on.

"With that packhoss and all, you'll be traveling like white folks," the Kid pointed out. "I'll be coming after you like an Injun."

With that he turned and walked into Belle's room. Crossing to the bed, he lay down on it as if meaning to snatch a short rest before leaving. If all went well, the Yankees would continue watching him, thinking Belle lay on the bed when all the time she made good her escape.

7

THAT'S NO WOMAN OVER THERE

"The Rebel Spy is in Matamoros," Abner Ffauldes told the woman who called herself Emily Corstin as she entered the dining room of the house facing the Confederate States' consulate shortly before eight o'clock in the evening.

Halting, Eve Coniston—the other name having been placed on the hotel's register to hide her true identity—stared at the leader of the United States Secret Service's Matamoros detachment.

"When did you learn that?" she demanded.

"Early this afternoon," Ffauldes replied. "I sent a message to you at the hotel. But you'd left and I didn't know where to find you."

Annoying though it might be, Eve could not argue on that point. After leaving the hotel, she had accompanied Charlie Kraus to start on part of the business that had brought her to Matamoros.

Events in the Mexican town, ranging from Belle Boyd's pre-

vious undetected arrival and departure to the Ysabel family's
wholesale smuggling activities, had caused serious doubts to be
raised in the U.S. Secret Service about the efficiency of
Ffauldes's detachment. So Eve Coniston had received orders to
investigate the matter while also trying to bring an end to the
smuggling.

Although shrewd, capable, efficient, and successful, Eve had
received little public acclaim and was hardly known beyond her
organization. The lack of recognition sometimes annoyed her,
but she also recognized its value. While Pauline Cushman received publicity, being boosted as the North's answer to Belle
Boyd, no mention of Eve ever reached the Yankee newspapers.
So she went her way unsuspected, achieving far more than the
so-called "Scout of the Cumberland's" often-told exploits.

From the little she had seen since her arrival aboard the
steam launches' depot ship, Eve knew she faced a formidable
task. Guided by Kraus, she rode some five miles upstream on
the Rio Grande's southern bank and talked with a number of
unsavory people who made their living along the bloody border
between Texas and Mexico. At the end of it she felt that she
was wasting her time. When Kraus brought up the matter of
reporting rebel troop movements, for money of course, all
agreed—even those who, she suspected, never crossed the river.
On the other matter discussed, the results had been far less
satisfactory. To be fair to him, Kraus had warned her from the
start about that.

When asked to spy on and report the movements of the
Ysabel family's smuggling trains, the border dwellers' attitudes
changed fast. A few refused profanely and point-blank. Others
seemed unwilling, frightened almost, to talk about it, and their
eyes took on a faraway look as they evaded even the question of
whether they had seen the Ysabels go by in the past. Only two
offered to help, and they did so with such blatant insincerity
that Eve doubted if anything would come of it.

On the way back to town she thought about the matter. Even
with the aid of the steam-launch flotilla, borrowed from the
Mississippi Squadron, catching the Ysabels in the act would be

anything but a sinecure. So she decided to concentrate her efforts at the source of the supply. The shipments brought into Matamoros could only arrive because some important French officials were looking the other way. If she produced proof against them, their superiors would be forced to make them carry out their duties correctly. Failing that, she could find evidence of Garfield helping the Ysabels and rebel spies. Then the U.S. consul could approach the French and demand that Garfield be ordered from the city for breach of diplomatic privilege. Causing the Confederate consul's removal ought to throw the landing organization into confusion long enough for the steam launches to learn the vagaries of the Rio Grande. Skilled veterans of the Mississippi campaign, they should be able to cope with the problems of blockading a smaller river.

Returning to the hotel, she found Ffauldes's message and visited him after eating with a French colonel who gave much helpful advice and a permit to travel after the curfew hour. She noticed the men keeping watch from the street on the Confederate consulate as her hired carriage drove up and learned the reason the moment she met Ffauldes.

Tall, lean, with a gaunt face that bore a mixture of assumed superiority and an avaricious nature, Abner Ffauldes wore a rumpled town suit and grubby shirt. His attitude showed that he resented the woman's presence. Like all liberal-intellectuals, Ffauldes hated any authority he did not wield himself. Eve Coniston had arrived the previous day with a letter from Pinkerton, giving her virtual control of the Matamoros detachment.

"Where is she now?" Eve asked, although willing to guess at the answer.

"Across the street there," Ffauldes replied. "We've had her under observation ever since she arrived. Well, soon after she arrived anyway."

"And how did she manage to reach the rebel consulate?"

"Dressed as a Mexican girl. Hell! She looked and dressed just like one and rode in on a donkey cart."

"You didn't expect her to come down the street in full Confederate Army uniform and waving the Stars and Bars, did you?" Eve said dryly, hoping her own uneasiness did not show.

All too well she remembered the Mexican girl at the hotel's plaza. Something about that whole affair had struck her as wrong from the start. The French sergeant showed, even unconscious, signs of greater agony than would arise from being pushed and falling over backwards to crack his head on the ground. Wishing to avoid becoming involved in French-Mexican affairs, she had kept her conclusions to herself. What if that terrified Mexican girl had really been—Eve did not care to take *that* line of thought any further. So she prevented herself from doing it by resuming the questioning.

"You're sure it was her?"

"Joe Giss and one of his men were over the wall, hidden in the grounds, and heard Garfield call her by name," Ffauldes answered. "As soon as he got out and told me, I put every available man to watching the house."

"You had a man in their garden?" Eve asked.

"And not for the first time," Ffauldes replied, smirking with smug satisfaction. "One or two of them go over the wall at night, using a leather pad against the broken glass, and lie up in the bushes all day."

"Our men?"

"They work for us. Either Joe Giss or one of his men go in."

"And what does it cost us?" said the practical Eve.

"Fifty dollars a day for one or both of them," Ffauldes answered, losing some of his smirk. "I'm making a list of French and other callers Garfield sees."

"And what they talk about?"

"Sometimes. Look, Giss and the other man take their lives in their hands every time they go over the wall."

"They're well paid for doing it," Eve pointed out. "Fifty dollars a day! Couldn't any of your own men—?"

"None of them have that kind of experience," Ffauldes told her sulkily. "It paid off today well enough. We know the Rebel's Spy's there."

What Ffauldes omitted to mention was the number of times

the watcher in the grounds had failed to bring back any worthwhile information. In his bigoted hatred of the supporters of the Confederacy who dared to oppose his own lofty ideals, Ffauldes overlooked the fact that the watching had, to that day, gained little more knowledge than was gathered by the normal lookouts outside the consulate's grounds. To know he was putting one over on the rebels satisfied him. What he did not know was that only rarely did Giss take the chance of entering the garden, or how most of the watching from within had been carried out by men with only a scanty knowledge of English. That Giss had gone in the previous night had been brought about by Eve's presence in the town. After meeting her, Charlie Kraus had warned his partner that there would need to be an improvement in their service if they hoped for it to continue. So Giss went in with the halfbreed and, in trying to gather some information of sufficient importance to satisfy Eve, had been discovered and lost his man while escaping.

"Have you seen her yourself?" Eve inquired, having formed a poor opinion of Joe Giss during their one brief meeting the previous evening.

"I saw her!" Ffauldes replied with considerably more enthusiasm than a mere glimpse of the South's top spy appeared to merit. "She's using a room at the front of the house, upstairs."

"And she's still there?"

"My men are covering the whole building, there's no way she could leave."

Before any more could be said, the door flew open and an excited-looking man dashed in.

"There's trouble across the river, Mr. Ffauldes!" he said. "We saw a flash, like an explosion, then rockets and flares started going up."

Darting to the window, Eve looked through it and saw the glow in the sky. She swung hurriedly to look at the men.

"Is the Rebel Spy still across the street?" she barked.

"Sure," the newcomer answered. "We saw her once at the dining-room window, wearing a fancy gown."

"How long since?" Eve asked.

"Maybe half, three quarters of an hour back," the man replied. "I'm near enough certain she's still in there. Garfield's been talking to somebody just now and I could see the hem of her dress from just in front of him."

"It may not be her," Eve said, half to herself. "I think she's here to— Come on, we'll go to the waterfront and see what we can learn."

"The curfew—!" Ffauldes croaked.

"I know about it!" Eve snapped. "The French won't enforce it on members of the U.S. consular staff going to see what's happening across the river."

"That's for sure," the lookout agreed. "They've never stopped us being out after curfew yet."

"Who's going with you?" Ffauldes asked.

"Leave the men on watch in the upstairs rooms and get the rest," Eve answered. "If the attack came from this side, I want whoever launched it."

"I'll go harness the coach," the lookout offered. "There're enough of the boys upstairs without me."

While Ffauldes gathered the men and his lookout prepared the coach, Eve went upstairs to interview the other watchers. She found all the men awake and showing considerable zeal in keeping the consulate under observation. However, none could state for certain that he had seen the Rebel Spy in the last three quarters of an hour or more.

"Shucks," one of them said. "She come up, put a frock on, and give her shirt and pants to a nigger maid for washing."

Listening to the man, Eve realized that the eager scrutiny of the other house had not been caused by news of her arrival. Taking a telescope, she lined it at the consulate and had the window of Belle's room pointed out. While it lay in darkness, she decided that its interior would be visible in daylight or with a lamp lit inside.

"You saw her?" Eve asked, repeating her opening question.

"And how," grinned the man. "She come in there dressed like a greaser. I saw her peeking out of the window. Must've figured we couldn't see into the room or weren't watching, 'cause she stripped, went for a bath, and when she come back we knew for sure she was the Rebel Spy."

"Why?"

"She got dressed in men's clothes. Dark shirt, riding breeches, like she's worn afore. Had a black wig on when she come in dressed like a greaser gal and under it she'd real short black hair."

"Could it have been a man dressed in woman's clothing?"

"Lady!" the lookout answered. "Believe me, that was no *man* I saw."

"You mean she stripped standing in front of the window?" Eve asked.

"Naw!" he replied, sounding just a touch disappointed. "Back by the bed. Must've figured we couldn't see that far into the room. But we could. Boy! Those app—* Well, we could see her good, *all* of her."

"Miss Coniston!" Ffauldes yelled from downstairs. "The coach's ready."

Although feeling doubts about what she had just heard, Eve put them aside. She could finish questioning the man later, but if they hoped to catch whoever had raided the shipping, a start must be made immediately.

Two men sat on the coach's box, while four more crammed inside with Ffauldes. No sooner had Eve climbed in than the driver started the two-horse team moving. Before they had covered half the distance, a French army patrol stopped them.

"United States consular staff," the driver replied in answer to the challenge. "We're going to—"

"*Monsieur!*" Eve called through the window, and the officer turned her way. "My husband is on a ship in Brownsville harbor. These gentlemen are taking me to see if all is well. I have a pass from Colonel Ponthieu."

"Of course, *madame*," the officer replied. "You may pass."

Continuing its journey through the streets, the coach came to a halt as close to the waterfront as the French would allow.

* Apples: slang for breasts.

Again an officer came up, a major this time, but he accepted the story of concern for the welfare of Eve's "husband" and raised no objection to the party going forward on foot.

"I want to take a boat out to the ships, Major," Eve went on, after acknowledging the permission. "Will that be possible?"

"It is on your own responsibility, *madame*," he answered.

Like all army officers and government officials, the major had received ambiguous instructions regarding his treatment of important *americanos del norte,* no matter which side in the war they served. Faced with the possibility of a long, arduous task in subduing Mexican resistance to their rule, the French high command dared not antagonize either the Confederate or federal governments. So they tended to order a blind eye turned to both sides' breaches of diplomatic conduct, or to be obliging to members of each.

More than that, Eve's request struck the major as being perfectly natural. Due to the prevailing conditions in Brownsville, with a hostile population waiting to rise against the occupying forces and constant harassment from Ford's command, the Yankee officers hesitated to bring in their wives. So a number of service families lived in Matamoros. Naturally they would be worried and wish to learn of their husbands' fate. Assuming Eve to be the wife of at least an army colonel or naval captain, the major decided she had been requested by the other wives to gather the required information.

Entering the boat accompanied by Ffauldes and another man, Eve set them to rowing across the river. The rest of her party spread out in an attempt to find the raiders.

Flares and lanterns illuminated the *Waterbury* and depot ship. From all appearances the raid had been at least a partial success. Water spurting out of hoses and the clanging of pumps aboard the *Waterbury* told of the fight to save her. Even as Eve's boat approached, she saw one of the forward Dahlgren nine-inch cannon tumble over the side through a gap cut in the bulwarks. A further gap at the stern told that the steam sloop's captain had jettisoned some of his armament in the bid to stay afloat. Yet, even with the reduction in weight of four—two from each side—9,200-pound cannon, the sloop lay low in the water. Beyond her, the depot ship listed far over to port and looked in a more sorry plight even than the *Waterbury*.

Kusik, the man rowing at Ffauldes' side, knew naval procedure, for he raised his voice in a hail. *"Waterbury* ahoy! Permission to come aboard!"

"Who the hell are you?" demanded an exasperated voice.

"If they're from some stinking newspaper, turn the hoses on 'em!" roared the burly captain, appearing at the rail.

"We're U.S. consular staff from Matamoros!" Ffauldes yelled hastily.

"Lay alongside aft and come aboard!" ordered the captain grudgingly, and Eve heard him continue in a lower tone, "A woman! That's all I need right now. A damned woman coming aboard asking stupid questions."

"I'll report him to the admiral comm—!" Ffauldes began.

"Shut your mouth!" Eve snapped. "He's right, but I have to go aboard."

She could sympathize with the captain, doing everything in his power to save his ship and faced by the arrival of what would probably amount to nothing more than useless sightseers. However, she wanted to learn if any of the raiders had been seen and might be identified.

Boarding the *Waterbury* presented no problem, for she lay low in the water. Two sailors reached through the gap in the bulwarks, caught Eve's wrists, and swung her up on to the deck. Kusik followed by his own efforts and Ffauldes struggled up after the other two.

"You understand I've no time to spare, madam," the captain told Eve, giving her a scowl along with the salute. "You may tell the ladies ashore that there've been no casualties in either vessel."

"Thank you, captain," she replied. "And the damage?"

"We're holed in the bottom, have plugged it with hammocks as best we can, but are still making water. The *Grayson* is in worse shape than us. I've had no report from her. You are from the consulate?"

"I'm with the Secret Service," Eve answered, her voice holding just a touch of pride. "Did anybody see the attackers?"

"See them!" growled the captain, sounding more angry than ever. "One of my officers had his hands on her and—"

"Her?" Eve prompted. "There was a woman involved?"

"Damn it, can't you see I'm—" the captain blared, then gave a resigned shrug. "Very well. It will come out later anyhow. Mr. Thurley. Lay aft here."

"Aye, aye, sir!" answered the abashed midshipman who had commanded the guard boat, running up to the party.

"Tell the lady about your outstanding achievement tonight, Mr. Thurley," ordered the captain. "And while you're at it, tell her about that damned wig you brought aboard with that blasted greaser down the coast last night. I'm going below to inspect the damage."

Slowly the midshipman told of Belle's "capture" and escape, clearly hating to admit his failure to civilians, especially when one of them was a woman. If he came out of the affair still retaining his commission, he would be lucky, and he knew it. So he spoke carefully, weighing each word with the view to how it would sound repeated before a court martial. Showing tact and using skilled questioning backed by sympathy, Eve drew out all the details.

"It could have happened to anybody," she finally said, with more compassion than she felt. The Rebel Spy had been in Yankee hands and escaped. No member of the U.S. Secret Service could regard that news with equanimity. However, she wished to let the young man down as lightly as possible in view of what his superiors would do to him. "What was that about a wig?"

Thurley did not hesitate with his answer. On that matter at least he could maintain a clear conscience, being covered in his actions by the captain's stringent orders.

"That was last night, ma'am. We heard shots from the shore and saw a fight by a fire. Captain sent me ashore with a party to investigate. The fighters ran before we landed. Hey, though! One of them was a woman—the same one we caught tonight,

I'll bet. At least they both had the same sort of short black hair.
The two men with her were Americans, frontiersmen from the
look of them."

"What baggage did they have?" Eve asked eagerly.

"Two trunks. They carried them off. The bigger man took
one and she helped the youngster with the other."

"And you didn't give chase?" Ffauldes put in.

"That was on Mexican territory, *mister,*" Thurley answered,
contempt for a civilian plain in his tone. "My orders were not
to go beyond the beach. I brought a greaser aboard with me,
but his jaw's smashed so bad that he can't talk."

"About what size were the trunks?" Eve inquired.

"About so," Thurley replied, demonstrating with his hands.
"I'd say they weighed around a hundred pounds each, the way
they carried them off."

Not large enough to carry two torpedoes, then, although that
proved little, Eve told herself. Then she looked at the young
officer and gave him a reassuring smile.

"There's nothing more you can tell us?"

"No, ma'am. Now I'd like to get back to my duties."

"Hell!" Kusik exclaimed, pointing. "Look there!"

Turning, they saw the *Grayson* lurch and then roll over until
she lay on her side. She took two of the launches with her,
smashing down on them before they could draw away, but the
other four hovered around her.

"Jettison two more cannon!" roared the captain, coming up
to the deck from below. "Move, damn you. Madam, I'd be
obliged if you'd go ashore, make contact with the Mex—
French authorities, and ask if I can run this ship in for repairs."

Brownsville did not offer many dockyard facilities. Nor did
Matamoros for that matter, but repairs could be carried out
more safely there. As long as the *Waterbury* made only such
repairs as would render her seaworthy and did not touch her
armament, she could enter a neutral port for that purpose under international law.

"I'll see the arrangements are made," Eve promised, knowing that the sloop would be safe in Matamoros even should

Brownsville be retaken by the Confederacy. "We'll get out from under your feet now, Captain."

While being rowed back to Matamoros, Eve turned over her findings in her mind and liked nothing about them. Somehow Belle Boyd's capture and escape seemed too fortunate, contrived almost. Then there had been her behavior in the Confederate consulate. After suspecting that her presence had been discovered, the Rebel Spy had acted in a peculiarly uncharacteristic manner. Not once but several times she had permitted herself to be seen, and in such a manner as to ensure a still more careful watch for her would be made. Eve could imagine how eagerly the lookouts had waited in the hope of seeing the girl disrobing again.

A spy as successful as Belle Boyd became cautious in the extreme. Of course she might be growing carelessly overconfident—but not if she had come to Matamoros on the business Eve suspected.

"Hurry!" Eve told the men.

"I'd say we're too late for that," Kusik answered. "The Rebel Spy's done what she came here for."

"I only hope you're right!" she breathed.

On the landing Eve found two of the men waiting to deliver a negative report. Telling one of them to stay and watch what happened across the river, she sent the other to pass the captain of the *Waterbury's* message to the U.S. consul. Then she went to the carriage and ordered Kusik to go as fast as he could to the house overlooking the rebel consulate.

At the house Eve threw herself from the coach and dashed inside. She ran up the stairs, bursting into the room where she had interviewed the lookouts earlier. One man lay dozing in a chair, but his companion sat at the window. Jolting awake, the first man joined his companion in meeting Eve's cold gaze with the hang-dog expressions caused by knowing that they had failed in their duty.

"She's back, Miss Coniston," the watcher announced. "Asleep on the bed."

"Damned if I can see how she got out," his companion went on.

"But she did!" Eve snapped. "I don't think Allan Pinkerton's going to like this at all."

Which, both men knew, was quite an understatement. There would definitely be a big reorganization of the Matamoros detachment when Eve Coniston reported to their leader.

"Yes'm," the watcher admitted. "It's not 'cause we didn't watch. Hell, we watched real good."

"Hoping to see her walk into that room there and strip off her clothes again, I suppose!" Eve shouted. "Anyway, I blame the men on the streets more than you in the houses. How was she dressed when she came back?"

"In a dark shirt and riding breeches. Looked like she'd been in the water!"

"She had!" Eve interrupted grimly. "And then?"

"She undressed," the man replied uneasily. "Dried herself and dressed in a black shirt and pants. We thought she aimed to go out, but she's lying on the bed."

"Did she leave the room at all?" Eve inquired, taking the telescope and focusing it on the room.

First she noticed that the curtains had been drawn down some of the way from the top of the window. Not enough to block all view of the interior, for she could see the shape on the bed.

"After she tried to pull down the curtain and it stuck," the man answered, "we figured she'd gone to get somebody to fix it, but nobody came."

"It stuck?" Eve repeated.

"Shucks," the second man protested. "We could still see her from the waist down, at least when she was on her feet, and she's there plain enough on the bed."

At that moment Kusik appeared at the door and Eve turned to him. "Describe the Ysabels to me!" she ordered.

"Father's a big, powerful feller. Black Irish from the looks of him."

"And the son?"

"Tall, slender as a beanpole. He looks about fourteen years old and innocent as a church full of choirboys—only don't let that fool you. Ffauldes hired a couple of Mexican *asesinos* to go after the Ysabels—he only tried it once."

"What happened?" Eve asked, lining the telescope again.

"We never did find out about one of them."

"And the other?"

"We found him leaning against the gate. His belly ripped wide open and an extra mouth—under his chin. After that there wasn't a hired killer would take on the chore. We hired Giss and Kraus in the first place hoping they would, or could, find men willing to try."

Most of the explanation passed unheeded as Eve stared at the room across the street. Everything fell into place and she realized the nature of the trick the Rebel Spy had played on them. Damaging though it had been, the raid on the shipping was only a diversion made to help the fiction that Belle Boyd was in the consulate building.

"That's no woman over there!" she snapped. "It's a young man, probably the Ysabel Kid!"

"Bu—But the clothes!" protested the watcher. "The Kid allus wears buckskins—"

"Except when he's dressed as a peon riding on a donkey cart, or a *vaquero* delivering a message!" Eve spat back. "Damn it, he can change clothes just like Belle Boyd did, although you probably wouldn't find the sight so attractive. And that's what's happened. While you've been sitting here watching him, the Rebel Spy has escaped again."

"Now she's done what she came here for, you mean?" Kusik put in.

"That's what she wants me to think," Eve answered. "Find Giss and Kraus for me as quickly as you can!"

"Yes'm!" answered the second of the watchers, to whom the order had been given, and he scuttled from the room.

"Mr. Kusik, be ready to leave in an hour," Eve went on, walking toward the door. "You'll be going up the Rio Grande with one of Kraus's men in a steam launch. I'll give you the necessary authority for the officer in command of the flotilla. I want the word spread that we'll pay a thousand dollars for the capture, alive if possible, of Sam Ysabel and the Rebel Spy."

"There's few enough, if anybody, who'll chance doing that, even for a thousand dollars," Kusik objected.

"Then spread the word that she and Ysabel are carrying a large sum, at least ten thousand dollars in gold, with them."

"It's a good story. Every border rat along the river will be looking for them when I spread it."

"I only wish it wasn't true," Eve thought as she started to walk down the stairs. "Because if they reach that damned renegade Klatwitter, it might easily cost us the war."

8

HE'S LUCKY TO STILL BE ALIVE

Barely had the door opened and Shafto entered the room when the Ysabel Kid came off the bed to face him. From full asleep, in more comfort than had come his way in many months, to wide awake took only a brief instant.

Across the street the man on watch let out a yell that brought his companion leaping to his side.

"The Coniston dame was right," the lookout said. "It's the Kid and not the Rebel Spy."

"Shafto bursting in like that, took with that feller we just saw go into the house," the second man replied, "I'd say means they know Miss Coniston left town with Giss and Kraus."

A point that Shafto was making to the Kid at that moment.

"They pulled out maybe three hours back, Lon. My man trailed along after them to try and learn what was up. Kusik from over there and one of Kraus's 'breeds left the others, heading toward the river. My man did as I said, stuck with the

Corstin woman. She went with Giss and Kraus to the Posada del Rio."

"That's Charlie's favorite hangout," the Kid drawled. "I wouldn't want to be caught dead in there—and you stand a chance of winding up that way even if you do no more than drink the *tequila* they serve."

"So I've heard," Shafto answered dryly. "Well, Kraus, the woman, and six of their men come out on good horses. From the way they look, they intended to go up river."

"Three hours back!" the Kid spat out. "Why in hell didn't your man—"

"They must've seen him. Two of Giss's men took after him and he's been trying to lose them ever since. He had to fight his way in, finally."

"There's times I talk a heap too much!" said the Kid contritely. "He's lucky to still be alive, tangling with Joe Giss's boys on their own ground."

"He caught a knife in the ribs doing it," Shafto replied. "Luckily he had a sword-stick and knew how to use it. Killed one of them and wounded the other. What do we do now?"

"I don't know about you," the Kid growled. "But I'm going after pappy to warn him. There's no point in trying to make 'em think Miss Belle's still here now."

"That's what I think. I've told the cook to make breakfast for you and put up food to take along."

"I'll take the breakfast. But forget the food. I've pemmican and jerked meat that'll last me and be lighter to carry. Which same I'll be moving fast. Say, I saw a right likely looking sorrel in the stables. Reckon I can borrow him to ride relay along with my ole nigger hoss?"

"Take him," Shafto offered, although the horse in question was his favorite mount. The Kid would need the best available animal, the way he must travel to reach his father in time. "Do you want me to go and saddle him?"

"Just a blanket'll do. If I can, I'll leave him someplace safe."

"Don't worry about the horse. Reaching Belle and your father's the important thing right now."

After the meal, the Kid and Shafto went to the stables. Although the youngster had brought his warbag to the consulate, he would not be taking it any farther. No Indian riding on a raiding mission cluttered himself up with spare clothing or anything but essentials, and the Kid intended to travel in such a manner. So he selected only a partly eaten *awyaw:t* of pemmican and a few strips of jerked buffalo meat, which could be rolled in the single blanket that would form his bed on the trail. For the rest, weapons and ammunition were his only other needs. Thirty rounds of soft lead balls for the Dragoon, fifty for the rifle, and a flask of powder would be sufficient. Every ounce of weight counted, so he decided against taking along the second Dragoon that lay in the warbag. While the revolver was of the Third Model, with a detachable canteen-carbine stock, the latter device did little to improve its potential for long-range shooting. In case of a fight from a distance, the Mississippi rifle would be more use. He dispensed with the rifle's saddleboot, intending to carry it in the lighter buckskin pouch presented to him by his grandfather on the day he rode out to fight the Yankees.

Saddling the stallion, he studied its black-patched hide and put aside his thoughts of changing out of the black clothing into his buckskins.

"Reckon you can find me a hat, Cap'n Rule?" he asked.

"I'll see what we have around," Shafto promised.

By the time he returned, the Kid was all ready to leave. The white stallion stood saddled and the sorrel bore a blanket Indian-fashion on its back, although with a white man's headstall, bit, and reins, the latter of the short, closed type favored by cavalrymen. The Kid's own reins were Texas-style, open in two separate straps, and he looped them loosely around the saddlehorn, knowing the white would stay by him tied or free.

Neither of the men realized as the Kid tried on the hats, and found a black Stetson to be the only one that fitted, that he had commenced wearing what would become his usual style of clothing. Only rarely in the years to come would the Kid wear other than all black clothes.

"Anybody watching the house, Cap'n?" the Kid inquired, swinging astride the sorrel with deft ease.

"Only the usual lookouts," Shafto replied. "Not that they'd try to stop you so close to the consulate. But they saw my man come in wounded. So they'll try it somewhere along the way."

"Likely," the Kid answered. "Somebody could get hurt if they try. Open up, Cap'n. I'm on my way."

Riding out of the gate, the Kid watched the Yankee-owned house but met with no trouble. Nor did he appear to attract any undue attention while riding through the town. Enough *americanos del norte* made Matamoros their home, coming and going in such a manner, to prevent his appearance from being out of the ordinary. However, the Kid did not relax. Any trouble that came his way in town would be unlikely to start in the better-class areas. Down among the *jacales* of the poor quarter was the danger area. More than one man entered that section and never returned, murdered for his weapons, horse, and clothing.

Holding his horses to a steady trot, the Kid noted the emptiness of the street leading on to the west-bound river trail. Instead of the normal swarm of children, men, and women gossiping in front of houses, he could see only two figures. Both wore the ragged clothes of ordinary peons and seemed to be following the age-old custom of *siesta*. The nearer man sat with his back against the wall of a *jacale*, sombrero drawn down over his face and serape hung negligently over his shoulder. Further along the street, the second of them took his rest standing with a shoulder propping him up against another adobe building.

Casually the Kid let his right hand fall to be thumb-hooked into the gunbelt close to the Colt's butt. It was a mite early for *siesta* hour, although diligent peons had been known to start before time on occasion. To the Kid's mind, the closer man at least was sitting just a touch too tense to be resting. More than that, his right hand lay under the serape and held a revolver. The Kid could see the glint of metal beyond the brown of the partially hidden hand. Nor did he miss the unobtrusive way the man inched up the sombrero and peeked from beneath its brim in his direction. However, after the one quick glance, the man appeared to relax. Then, as the Kid came closer, the man took another look. A startled croak broke from him and he began to lurch erect, bringing the revolver into view.

Even as the Kid twisted his old Dragoon from its holster, he guessed what had happened. Coming from the east, with the morning sun behind him, he at first had not been recognized by the man. Riding the sorrel, with the stallion's white coat bearing the black patches still, dressed in the black clothing instead of his usual buckskins, all helped the deception. Recognition came a fatal minute too late for the man, one of Joe Giss's regular helpers. Flame belched from the Dragoon's muzzle and the lead ball drove, by accident rather than lenient aim, into the man's shoulder. Not that the wound it caused could be termed slight, for a soft lead ball opened up on impact and caused tissue damage out of all proportion to its size. Stumbling back, the man let his revolver fall from a hand he would never use again.

At the shot the second man threw off his pretense of sleeping. He lunged away from the building, bringing a Colt into view. The Kid saw him as a greater threat than the first would-be attacker. No Mexican, to whom a gun took second place to the knife, but an American—despite the clothes—and one who knew how to handle a revolver.

Some thirty yards separated them, hardly ideal revolver-fighting range. However, the man did not hesitate. No matter how he dressed, the Ysabel Kid could not be trifled with at such a moment. With that thought in mind, the man raised the Colt shoulder high, sighted, and fired.

An instant before the Colt barked, the Kid brought the sorrel to a halt, tossed his right leg forward over its neck, and dropped to the ground. The bullet cut the air where his body had been a moment earlier. On reaching the ground, the Kid sank immediately into a kneeling position, left elbow resting on the raised knee and supporting the right hand as he aimed the old Dragoon. Before the man recocked his Colt, the Dragoon bellowed. Lead, driven by forty grains of powder—the most powerful loading possible at that time in a handgun—smashed into the man. Flung backward, he crashed into the wall of the *jacale* and bounced from it. In falling, he lost his hat and it rolled out into the street.

Rising, the Kid darted a quick glance around him. While he saw no sign of enemies, voices raised in the *jacale* behind his first victim told of their presence. So he ran toward the restlessly moving sorrel and leap-frog mounted its back, setting it running while thrusting away the Colt. Bursting out of the *jacale,* the leader of two men threw a shot after the departing Kid and might have made a lucky hit but for one thing. Having need for it at a later time, the Kid leaned sideways from the racing sorrel and scooped up the sombrero dropped by the disguised American. Doing so saved his life, for the bullet hissed just above him as he moved. In passing he looked at the dead man and recognized him as one of the many who lived along the bloody border by any means available.

"Trust Joe to move fast," the Kid mused as he urged the sorrel on, the white stallion sticking close to his side. "He must've hired that cuss as soon as he got the word."

Another bullet made its eerie sound as it hummed by his head. Then he turned a corner, which hid him from the shooters. To his ears came the yelled order to get the horses *pronto.*

"Which same means I'm not out of the woods by a long Texas mile," the Kid told himself. "Ole Joe's likely waiting up the trail with more of 'em. Leastwise, I'll be mortal offended happen he figures *four* of 'em was all he needed to take me."

Passing beyond the last buildings of the town, the Kid turned and saw two riders following. However, knowing him to be Cabrito, they made no attempt to come too close. That they followed at all suggested they expected Giss and more help to be waiting somewhere ahead.

The point of importance being, where would the reinforcements lay their ambush?

Not too far from town, the Kid figured. Close enough to hear shooting and make preparations in case the first attempt at stopping him failed. Too far away and he might turn off the trail to head across country. Prudence dictated that he follow that line of action; but the Kid could not claim prudence among his many virtues.

So he continued to ride along the trail, counting on his trained senses to locate the waiting men. During his childhood he had always excelled at the game of *Nan-ip-ka,* Guess-Over-the-Hill, by which Comanche boys learned to locate hidden enemies. Nor had he ever forgotten the skills gained in those formative years.

At first he rode through fairly open country unsuitable for the laying of an ambush, especially with Cabrito, the Ysabel Kid, as the proposed victim. However, about a mile from town the trail entered and wound through thickly wooded country.

Looking ahead, he saw a small cart drawn across the trail, its shafts empty and no sign of the driver. So he turned in time to see one of the following men making an obvious signal, which ended abruptly on noticing he was being observed.

"Down there, huh," he grinned, eyes raking the ground around the wagon.

A white man might have betrayed himself through anxiety or overeagerness, but never a *Pehnane tehnap,* and the Kid was all of that as he continued to ride into the ambush. No longer did he look young or innocent. Lips drawn back in a wolfish grin, rest of face a cold, savage mask, he might have been Long Walker, war leader of the dreaded Dog Soldier lodge, heading to meet an enemy.

Not that he underestimated the dangers of the situation. Joe Giss claimed few peers in accurate rifle shooting and—as the Kid had told Shafto—had learned the art of concealment from Indians. So he would be hard for even a *Pehnane* to locate. Anywhere within three hundred yards of the cart could be the danger area. Up to that distance Giss allowed to be able to knock out a squirrel's eye and call which one he meant to hit.

"So it's from now to maybe a hundred and not less'n fifty," the Kid decided, gauging the distance with an eye almost as accurate as a surveyor's tape measure. "Come on, Joe. Show your skinny-gutted hand. There's one of your boys, all hid real

careful behind that pepperwood tree. Another hunkered under
the deadfall and one laid up between them sassafrass bushes.
Where're you, Joe? Come out, come out, wherever you are."

Giving no sign that he had located three of his enemies, the
Kid rode on. Still no hint of Giss's presence. Yet he would be
there, hidden carefully and squinting along the sights of his
rifle.

Watching the Kid draw closer, the man behind the pepperwood tree grew more alarmed. That was no ordinary man
approaching, but Cabrito, who many claimed to have a
charmed life. Gomez had been an *asesino* of high quality,
skilled at his work, and everybody knew how he had died when
sent after the Ysabel Kid. So, despite Giss's orders that the
others wait until he opened fire, the Mexican acted. Burning
powder sparked alongside the pepperwood tree and the Kid
slid sideways between the two horses.

"I got him!" yelled the man, his voice almost drowned out by
other shots.

Finger already squeezing the Sharps rifle's trigger, Joe Giss
had received a shock when the Mexican's shot cracked out.
Nor could he control the involuntary tightening of his forefinger that set the rifle's mechanism working. Both his remaining
men's weapons barked almost at the same moment and the
three bullets tore harmlessly over the backs of the approaching
horses.

Carefully concealed under the branches of another sassafrass
bush, Giss heard his man's exultant yell. At first glance the
words appeared to be justified, for the horses raced down the
trail with no sign of a rider. The trouble being that the Kid's
body did not lie on the trail either. In which case, the Sharps
ought to be reloaded and fast. Which raised a snag. To load a
rifle, even a breech-feeding Sharps, meant movement sure to
draw the Kid's attention to Giss's hiding place. Attracting
Cabrito's interest at such a moment was as dangerous a pastime
as poking one's head into the mouth of a starving silvertip
grizzly bear and saying "Bite it."

Whoops of delight rose from Giss's less perspicacious companions, and he could see that none of them thought to reload their rifles. Then they too realized that something must be wrong. The two men from town signaled violently, and not in congratulation for a well-aimed shot. Closer thundered the two horses, still with no sign of the Kid. So the ambushers belatedly reached for powder flasks to begin the business of recharging their rifles.

When he slid from the sorrel's back, a split second before the Mexican cut loose at him, the Kid caught hold of the white's saddlehorn. He hung suspended between the two horses, guiding the white by word and signal while retaining his hold of the sorrel's reins. Watching ahead, he saw the cart rushing nearer.

"Sorry, Cap'n Rule," he breathed. "But I don't know if I can trust your hoss to come with me."

With that, he let the reins free to hang over the borrowed horse's neck. Dropping his feet to the ground, he used their impact to bound up and astride the white's saddle. A wild Comanche yell shattered the air and the huge horse lengthened its stride. Dropping his rifle, one of the Mexicans sprang from his cover and snatched at the holstered revolver on his hip. None of the others were even close to being reloaded and could only stare, hoping not to catch the Kid's eye.

Up soared the white stallion, taking the cart like a hunter-spooked white-tail deer bounding over a bush. Gathering itself, the sorrel also jumped, clearing the obstacle and lighting down running alongside the white. Wanting his own horse as fresh as possible for the work ahead, the Kid quit its saddle, dropped to the ground, and leapt onto the sorrel's back once more. Although the Mexican drew and fired his revolver, the bullet came nowhere near hitting the fast-moving Kid.

"Get after him, you stinking greasers!" Giss howled, rolling out from under the bush and standing up.

Under the pretense of reloading the Sharps, Giss allowed his men to reach their horses—hidden among the trees—first. By the time he completed the loading, they were mounted and starting after the Kid. However, his plan failed, for once by the cart they drew rein and waited for him. Scowling, he rode up and ordered the chase to be continued. Giss never cared to take chances—and neither did his men where the Ysabel Kid was concerned.

Holding his horses to a gallop, the Kid watched for a chance to lose his pursuers. At first he stuck to the trail, not wishing to pass through that thickly tangled woodland when riding at speed. A mile or so fell behind him before he reached more open country. So far his hunters had caught only fleeting glimpses of him on the winding trail and wasted no lead in trying for such a scanty target. However, the trail stretched straight and level for almost a quarter of a mile. That meant presenting Joe Giss with too good a mark at which to aim. So the Kid swung his horses from the trail, riding up the slope flanking it to the south through the scattered trees and bushes.

Just as he reached the top, something struck the sorrel. The Kid heard the horse's stricken grunt and the sound of a shot from behind him. Then the sorrel staggered and began to collapse. Throwing his leg across its back, he jumped clear and darted around the white stallion's rump. Even using the Indian-made boot, the Kid carried his rifle Texas fashion, on the left of the saddle with the butt pointing to the rear. So he needed only to grip the wrist of the butt and the horse walking away slid the rifle free.

"That Kid's luckier'n the devil!" Giss spat out, lowering his smoking Sharps.

Seeing the Kid approaching the top of the slope and realizing the nature of the country beyond it, Giss felt disinclined to follow the young Texan further. So he swung up his Sharps and chanced a snap shot. At almost a hundred yards, on a fast-moving target, he might have counted himself fortunate to come so close to hitting his mark.

Swiveling around, the long old Mississippi rifle flowing to his shoulder, the Kid sighted quickly and took a fast shot. Giss's hat spun from his head and he threw himself from the saddle to dive into cover, a move his men copied with some speed. Once hidden from further bullets, they looked to their leader for guidance. Not for almost two minutes did Giss offer to give any. Then he looked up the slope and sucked in a breath.

"Let's go. Stay with the hosses, Manuel. The rest of us'll foot it."

After shooting, the Kid ran to where his stallion was waiting. He thrust the rifle unloaded into the boot and took the sombrero collected in Matamoros from where it hung on the saddlehorn. Drawing his bowie knife, he slashed open the top of the crown and ripped the brim. Tossing the ruined hat on to the body of the sorrel, he turned, mounted the white, and rode off to the southwest.

Advancing cautiously up the slope, darting from cover to cover, Giss and his men approached the dead horse. Halting, their gaze went to the sombrero and noted the damage. Then they exchanged glances as the significance of what they saw struck them. All of the men, including Giss, had worked with *Comanchero* bands and knew something of Comanche Indian ways—enough to read the message left by the Kid.

If a raiding *Pehnane* brave found enemies persistently sticking to his trail, seeking to regain the loot lifted from them, he would destroy an item of their property and leave it in his tracks. That served as a warning of his future intentions. No longer would he content himself with passive flight. If they continued beyond his marker, he would kill on sight.

Some people, considering the Kid's youth and appearance of innocence, might have regarded the hat as mere ostentation left without serious intent, but Giss did not number among them. He *knew,* as sure as spring followed winter, that to follow the dark youngster would be courting quick, unexpected death. So Joe Giss reached a rapid decision.

"That frog-eater colonel in Matamoros wants somebody to scout for him, boys," he announced. "I conclude it'd be easy money. Let's go take on for him."

That meant deserting his partner, but Charlie Kraus had an understanding nature. Anyway, if their expressions were any guide, Giss's companions wholeheartedly approved of the desertion, even if scouting for the French meant working against their own people. Turning, they walked back down the slope, collected their horses, and retraced their tracks to Matamoros.

9

KEEP YOUR HANDS OFF MY
PERFUME

"Tired, Miss Boyd?" Sam Ysabel asked, turning in his saddle and studying their backtrail.

"I've forgotten what a bed is," she replied with a wry smile and eased her aching limbs as best she could.

"Rosita O'Malley's place's down this ways a piece," Ysabel told her. "We'll stop off and let the horses rest a spell. You can grab some sleep till nightfall and then we'll push on again."

"I'll not argue on that," Belle assured him.

Before Eve Coniston returned to the house, Belle and Shafto had slipped away from the consulate. They carried the heavy saddlebags, containing the money, a change of clothing, and a few other items Belle felt she might need, with them. Joining Sam Ysabel at the prearranged rendezvous, the girl rode out of Matamoros before midnight. All through the night and on toward the following noon they continued to ride at a good pace. Although Belle felt very tired, she refused to show it until Ysabel suggested that they should halt.

At first sight Rosita O'Malley's cantina and *posada* looked little different from hundreds of other such places scattered through the Rio Grande border country. A two-story adobe building set on the banks of a small stream, it offered a choice of stables or corrals for its guests' horses. Choosing the former, Ysabel led the way inside.

"Only Rosita's hosses here, and at the corral," he commented, and his grulla walked into a stall in a manner that showed that it had often done so before.

Fighting down her tiredness, Belle set to work tending to her bay. Then she went to help Ysabel care for the packhorse. Brought along more as a blind than for any other reason, the packs were empty and held in shape by light frameworks of twigs. While working on the horse, she saw a shadow at the doors and looked around. A tall, buxom, black-haired woman, good-looking although no longer in the bloom of youth, entered. She wore a plain black dress, although of more daring cut than convention allowed. The woman halted, and her smile of welcome died as her eyes turned from Ysabel to Belle.

"*Hola,* Rosita gal," Ysabel greeted.

"Who's she, Big Sam?" the woman demanded in English.

"Fee-ancy to one of Jack Cureton's Rangers, come down the coast by boat. I'm taking her up to meet him."

"You sure on that?"

"Would I lie to you, Rosey gal?" asked Ysabel, sounding pained. "Come here and give a hard-traveled man a kiss."

A request to which Rosita responded with gusto, although throwing Belle a challenging, defiant glare as she commenced. When released, she turned to face the girl once more.

"Who's your feller, sister?"

"Solly Cole from up Tyler way," Ysabel put in. "Go make us some food, and we'll want two rooms until nightfall."

"I think you're one big liar, Sam Ysabel," Rosita stated. "And if I thought what I was thinking's true, I'd alter the shape of her face some."

"You mean like this?" asked Belle, swinging gracefully into a *chassé,* rear lateral kick, which slashed her foot hard into the wall of the stall.

Jerking back a pace, Rosita stared at the mark on the wall and noted it to be at the height of her own face. Nor did she overlook the power with which the kick had landed, and she realized what it would do should it strike home on human flesh. A grin came to her face.

"I hope you 'n' Solly Cole'll be happy, *señorita,*" she said. "And I still reckon Big Sam's a liar."

"Only about me," Belle smiled back. "He's loyal and true to you."

"Yeah. I just bet he is," Rosita replied. "As long as he's where I can keep both eyes on him. Come on. Leave the big *Indio* to finish the work and I'll give you a meal. Then you look like you could use some sleep."

Clearly the woman accepted that Belle and Ysabel were traveling together without romantic intentions. However, she asked no questions about the girl's real reason for riding the river trail. Nobody, not even a close friend like Rosita O'Malley, inquired too closely into the Ysabel family's business—not twice hand-running, anyways.

"Shall I keep the saddlebags, or you, Miss Belle?" Ysabel asked.

"You, although there are a couple of things I'd like from them before I go to sleep," the girl replied.

For a *posada* drawing its trade from people traveling the bloody border, Rosita's place offered a good standard of cleanliness, and the bed in the room allocated to Belle looked comfortable. Tired though she might be, Belle collected her dark blue shirt and riding breeches—dried and ironed hurriedly before she left the consulate—her parasol, and to Ysabel's amusement, a perfume bottle with its spray attached from the saddlebags before going to catch up on her rest. She closed the door, placed her property on the bedside chair, hung her gunbelt on its back, and eased off her boots. Then she lay on the bed and went to sleep.

Practice had taught Belle to wake at any given time. When

she opened her eyes, feeling refreshed, she saw that the sun hung low in the western sky. Rising, she worked her muscles and found the ache had left them. It would be time to move soon, so she started to change clothes. While the black shirt and trousers fitted her, they lacked the comfortable feel of her older garments. With the riding breeches and boots on, a precaution against sudden departure, Belle reached for the shirt. She heard the lock click, and the door opened.

"Well, now, ain't that a sight to see?" asked an unfamiliar male voice.

Swinging around, Belle saw a man and woman entering the room. Strangers to her, they wore filthy clothes and gave an impression of voluntary uncleanliness. Across the passage a man covered Sam Ysabel at the door to his room and a third turned toward the speaker.

"Wha—!" Belle began, darting a glance toward her gunbelt.

"You try it and I'll blow your purty head off, gal!" warned the man at the door, thrusting forward a Le Mat revolver in a threatening manner. "Go take her gun, Amy-Jo."

Standing at the opposite end of the bed to her weapons, Belle knew she could not hope to reach them in time. She stood still as the young woman walked by her and the man came closer. Despite his eyes ogling her bare shoulders and revealing underskirt, the Le Mat never wavered from its line on her stomach.

"Well I swan, Hickey!" Amy-Jo announced, picking up the perfume bottle. "If she don't have some fancy scent 'long."

"Keep your hands off my perfume!" Belle snapped.

"You hear her, Hickey?" Amy-Jo asked. "Anybody'd think it was her got the gun way she gives orders."

"Don't you put any of that perfume on yourself!" Belle warned.

"Listen here now, quality gal!" Amy-Jo flared back. "Right now I don't have to do one li'l thing you tells me."

With that she directed the nozzle at her face and squeezed the bulb. A misty spray of liquid shot out, striking just under her nose. Instantly Amy-Jo let out a strangled, gagging croak, half-dropping, half-throwing the bottle onto the bed as she reeled backward. The raw, acrid aroma of ammonia rose from the girl as she stumbled around in a circle and dropped, fighting for breath, to her knees.

Hickey's head jerked around to stare at Amy-Jo and for a moment he wondered what had caused the girl to act in such a manner. After which he became too engrossed in his own problems to care.

Up rose Belle's foot, and this time she wore a boot highly suitable for kicking. While Hickey's Le Mat wavered involuntarily out of line, the toe of Belle's boot drove with considerable power under his jaw. Shooting backward across the room, he crashed into the wall, bounced from it, and landed facedown on the floor.

At the commotion, the nearer of the men in the passage turned and sprang into Belle's room. His companion foolishly failed to keep full attention on Sam Ysabel. Whipping across, Ysabel's right hand slapped the man's revolver aside and flashed toward his holstered Dragoon. As the man took an unintended pace to the rear, Ysabel bunched and launched his left fist against the side of the other's head. Sent reeling across the passage, the man tried to bring his gun back into line. Thumb-cocked on the draw, the big Dragoon bellowed in Ysabel's hand as it cleared leather. The bullet sliced into the man's head, immediately ending his attempt at shooting. Even before the man fell, Ysabel went leaping toward the door of Belle's room.

Diving onto the bed as Hickey's second companion entered, Belle grabbed the scent spray. She swung its nozzle toward the man as he lunged with hands reaching for her, and squeezed the bulb. Caught in the face by the spray of ammonia, the man duplicated Amy-Jo's reactions. Belle brought up her foot, ramming it into his stomach and shoving hard. Propelled backward, the man offered Ysabel a tempting target. Up and down rose the big Texan's arm, smashing the base of the Dragoon's butt on top of the man's head to drop him like a poleaxed steer.

From downstairs came the voice of Rosita O'Malley, raised in a mixture of lurid Spanish and Irish curses.

"Watch 'em, gal!" Ysabel yelled, turning to dash out of the room and in the direction of the stairs.

Looking around her, Belle decided there would be no need to bother about the visitors for a spell. Even Amy-Jo showed no signs of recovery, but still crouched on the floor gagging and trying to breathe.

"I warned you not to use it," Belle remarked as she picked up her shirt.

Deciding that they would be making a hurried departure, Belle donned the shirt, tucked it into her waistband, and then strapped on the gunbelt. With the Dance at her hip she felt capable of dealing with anything Hickey's crowd cared to start. Gathering up her belongings, she took them to Ysabel's room. On coming out, she saw Ysabel returning. The big Texan walked toward her, shaking his head as if unable to believe what he had found below.

"I never figured Hickey to have one li'l bit of right good sense," he told the girl. "But I never reckoned he'd be hawg-stupid enough to leave just *one* feller guarding Rosey."

"Is she all right?" Belle asked.

"She's fine. Only I don't know how the feller'll feel when he gets round to feeling again. That skillet she hit him with sure messed up his face some."

From which Belle concluded that Rosita had managed to cope with the situation unaided.

"What lousy luck," Belle commented. "Picking today of all times to attempt a robbery."

"Like I say," Ysabel drawled, "Hickey's not smart, but he's a whole heap too smart to try a game like that at Rosey's place and again' me without real good reason. If he knowed how much money we're carrying—"

"Then he might?"

"He just might get brave enough then."

"But he can't know!" Belle stated.

"He *shouldn't* know," corrected Ysabel. "Maybe we'd best ask some questions!"

"I think you're right," Belle agreed. "The girl looks to be the only one likely to tell us anything for a time."

Sucking in sobbing breaths of air, Amy-Jo stared with tear-reddened, frightened eyes as Belle and Ysabel approached her.

"We didn't mean no harm!" the girl whined, edging across the floor on her rump away from them and darting a glance at her companions. "I tried to tell Hickey it wouldn't work."

"What wouldn't work, Amy-Jo?" Ysabel asked.

"Nothin'."

Bending down, Belle dug her fingers into the girl's dirty hair and jerked her head back, looking at Ysabel and saying, "Pass me that scent bottle, please, Sergeant Ysabel."

"No!" Amy-Jo yelped, the recollection of her first tangling with the thing still vivid in her mind.

"What wouldn't work?" Belle demanded.

"H-Hickey'd kill me if he knowed I'd talked!" Amy-Jo wailed.

"You've got troubles from all sides, gal," Ysabel told her unsympathetically. "Rosita's all riled up and lookin' to take it out of somebody's hide. I'll just call and tell her you're the first one woke up."

"Lookee, Big Sam!" the girl yelped, fear plain on her face as she directed another glance at the still form of her leader. "I had to come. You know Hickey!"

"I know him," Ysabel admitted. "And I never figured he'd be *loco* enough to try a game like this."

"That ten thousand dollars you've got sounded mighty tempting," Amy-Jo answered simply.

Belle and Ysabel exchanged glances. Maybe the sum fell short of the actual total, but it came close enough to arouse ugly suspicions.

"How'd you know about that?" Ysabel growled.

"We was down on the river this afternoon," Amy-Jo replied. "Heard somethin' comin' and dog my cats if'n around a bend don't steam three itty-bitty boats like I've never seed afore. Like big rowin' boats they was, only with chimneys 'n' engines in 'em. Done got cannons in the front—"

"Steam launches!" Belle breathed. "What about them?"

"We was just fixin' to get the hell out of there when a feller yells out Hickey's name. It was Golly, that 'breed who rides for Charlie Kraus. Tells us it's all right and they only wants to make talk."

"What did he say?" Belle asked.

"That Big Sam was comin' upriver with you and for us to go after you. Hickey wouldn't've listened, only Golly allowed you'd got maybe ten thousand in gold along. Said for us to let Charlie have a cut if we got it."

"Who were in the boat?"

"Fellers in uniforms, ma'am. They let Golly come onto the bank to talk to us; that's how he let on about the money."

"Smart," Belle said to Ysabel. "They're sending word upriver and making it look like the people he tells are getting something extra that the Yankees don't know about."

"Smart and tricky," Ysabel agreed. "Charlie Kraus always was. What come off next, Amy-Jo?"

"Golly gets back to the boat and they heads on upriver," the girl replied. "Then Hickey allows you'd be sure to call in here, Big Sam, and we should oughta try for the money. Only it didn't work."

"You tell Hickey, when he starts to take notice, to keep well out of my sight from now on," Ysabel growled.

"If you ain't holdin' me, I'm gonna be long gone afore that," the girl stated. "Hickey's not gonna forget it was me worked that damned scent squirter."

"Light out, gal," Ysabel grinned. "Let's get goin', Miss Belle."

Collecting their belongings, Belle and Ysabel went downstairs. By the time they reached the ground floor, the drumming of hooves told that Amy-Jo had made good her promise of departing.

"I let her go," Rosita remarked.

"She'd not help against Hickey," Ysabel answered. "So it's as well."

"I'm sorry about making trouble for you, Rosita," Belle went on.

"So'll Hickey be, unless you killed him," the woman replied, nodding to a bunch of tough-looking Mexicans who hovered in the background. "We'll tend to everything here. You'd best start riding."

"Could be there'll be more folks around asking about us, Rosey," Ysabel warned. "Don't get smart should they come."

"They'll get the same as everybody else," Rosita promised. "Food, a place to sleep, and no information. How about Lon?"

"Tell him we're headed south, instead of stickin' to the river trail," Ysabel replied. "He'll find us easy enough."

"I agree with you, Sergeant," Belle put in. "Those launches can make easily six miles an hour going upriver and will have been moving while we rested."

"They've got engines that don't get tired, ma'am," the Texan pointed out. "Hosses do, and people. Thing is, how did the Yankees get to know about us?"

"They have efficient spies too," Belle replied as they walked out of the building. "I've been afraid they'd find out from the start."

"You mean they brought them launches here especial for this?"

"No. Although somebody acted fast and smart in using them to pass on the message. I don't suppose there's a chance of them meeting some of our troops along the river?"

"Devil the bit this far from Brownsville."

"How about Captain Cureton and his men?" Belle asked.

"They're Rangers, not army. Fellers who didn't want to take sides, some Yankees and some of us rebs," Ysabel explained. "Cureton can only hold 'em together by stayin' clear of either side in the war. They're tryin' to protect the homes of soldiers away fightin' from Injuns, bad whites, and Mexican *bandidos*. There'll be no help from them."

"And the man with the launches can find other men like Hickey?"

"Or worse. Golly knows the river hangouts. Even if he only

tells 'em ten thousand dollars, there'll be plenty wantin' to try for it."

"What do we do, then?" Belle inquired.

"Like I said. Go south. They'll likely all be figuring on us sticking to the river and looking for a place to cross into Texas."

"How about Rosita?" Belle said as she saddled her horse. "Will she be safe after we've gone?"

"From Hickey?" Ysabel laughed. "She could eat two like him and his whole bunch. And for the rest—well, she's got kin on both sides of the river, tough *hombres* all of 'em, thicker'n fleas on an Injun dawg, who'll come a-runnin' happen she yells, or should anything untoward happen to her. Yes, ma'am. I figure Rosey'll be all right. But we sure as hell won't, unless we put some miles between us and the border."

10
YOU NEVER SHOULD'VE
TRIED A KNIFE

Seeing a dead animal on the range, a domesticated dog will go straight up to it and investigate. A wolf never does, but circles around the body warily, alert for traps and danger.

So it was with the Ysabel Kid as he rode toward Rosita O'Malley's place at ten o'clock on the night of his father's hectic visit. Instead of riding up to the buildings—owned by a good and loyal friend though they might be—he studied them from a distance and made a circle around to take note of everything. Lights glowed at the downstairs windows and he could see a number of horses in the corral.

Slipping from the white's saddle, he led it to some trees beyond the house. Although he removed the headstall and bit, hanging them with the coiled rope on the horn, he left the saddle in place. The horse would remain where he left it, tied or free, while a whistle would bring it to him when needed. So he left it in the cover of the trees, with good grazing under foot. Silently as an owl hunting in the night sky, the Kid advanced on foot toward the buildings. His route took him by the corral, and he kept down wind as a matter of simple precaution. Pausing, he looked the horses over. Fine animals, yet their assortment of colors seemed to rule out a French cavalry patrol. Which still left a whole slew of possibilities. No guards around the place made the visitors unlikely to be Juaristas, for such invariably kept watch for their foreign enemies. That left a variety of border citizens, not all friendly to the Ysabel family, who might be calling on Rosita O'Malley.

The Kid moved on, creeping to the side of the main building and moving to where he could see into the big barroom through a window. What he saw surprised him and made him bless the precautions taken.

The visitors formed two distinct groups, either of which might be found anywhere along the bloody border, except in areas with large and efficient law-enforcement organizations. Finding them both at Rosita O'Malley's place, noted for its neutrality in the various border feuds, might have been natural enough. What surprised the Kid was the fact that the two leaders shared a table in apparent amity.

No mere chance meeting could bring them together, nor a desire to discuss matters of cultural interest. Tall, slender, elegantly dressed like a wealthy *haciendero*, Ramon Peraro possessed leanings toward education and gentlemanly habits. Which same nobody could even start to claim for Bully Segan. Big, bulky, with cold, hard eyes practically the only thing visible among his mat of whiskers, he wore buckskins and might have been a member of the old hairy Rocky Mountain brigade who opened up so much of the far West. Only one thing linked Peraro and Segan. Each ran as mean a band of cutthroats and killers as could be assembled.

Four of Segan's men, *americanos del norte* dressed in buckskins and well armed, sat at a table behind their boss. While two of Peraro's gang stood at the bar, another four sat over against the wall beyond the *bandido* leader. The atmosphere seemed strained, only natural with the two gangs in competition with each other, and most of the company drank left-handed. Only the two leaders sat together, using the right hand to raise their *tequila* glasses. Watching the others, the Kid was reminded of seeing, as a boy, a cougar and grizzly bear drinking on either side of the only waterhole in ten miles. The two predators showed the same alert, suspicious watchfulness as did the members of the rival gangs.

"Now, what in hell's ole Bully Segan doing sat here all friendlied up with Peraro?" the Kid asked himself. "Last I heard, Ramon was fixing to side with Juarez against the French."

Not to celebrate, or merely have fun, certainly, for the men ignored Rosita's girls and drank sparingly. One possibility sprang to mind. Ever since they started smuggling, long before the war, the Ysabels had built up a name for rugged, effective defense of their property. Few gangs on the border would chance attacking one of their pack trains. Yet it seemed unlikely that such a project would bring together Peraro and Segan. Even less so that their meeting would take place at Rosita O'Malley's *posada*, known to be the Ysabel family's favorite visiting spot.

Deciding to learn more about the visitors before entering, the Kid withdrew and went to the rear of the building. He could see into the kitchen, but made no attempt to approach it. Instead he settled on his haunches and waited in the darkness with all the patience of his maternal grandfather's people.

Almost an hour passed before Rosita entered the kitchen and came close enough to its open door for the Kid's purpose. Cupping his hands around his mouth, he gave a near perfect imitation of an Arizona pyrrhuloxia's mating call. Passing the doorway, Rosita changed direction and walked outside. Again came the twittering whistle. Aware that the bird rarely came into that region and sang only in daylight, she knew the call to be a signal. So she spoke over her shoulder, telling the cook she was going out back, and walked into the darkness.

"Cabrito?" she asked, speaking barely above a whisper.

"It ain't Benito Juarez," the youngster replied, moving to her side. "You got the cream of so-ciety tonight, Rosey."

"That's no way to talk about my customers," the woman answered, lowering the Remington Double Derringer she had carried concealed on her person since Sam Ysabel's departure. "Way you're fancied up, I thought you'd be coming in. All it wants is for your pappy and that high-quality gal to come along for it to be the success of the year."

A grin twisted the Kid's lips as he realized that his change of clothes had come close to bringing a bullet into his belly. Knowing Rosita, he did not doubt that she would have shot if he had spoken less promptly to identify himself. Not that he blamed her. Anybody who aroused the suspicions of either Peraro or Segan stood a better than fair chance of meeting a painful death. So she could take no chances.

"What's up, Rosey?" he asked, moving to one side as she entered the small backhouse and left its door open.

"I don't know who that high-quality gal was, or what she's doing; and'd's soon not find out," Rosita answered. "But she's sure got a heap of real nice folks looking for her and Big Sam."

"Charlie Kraus here as well as Segan and Peraro?"

"Nope. Hickey 'n' his crowd come in earlier. Lone Walt's still here—'fact he won't be leaving."

"Poor ole Lone Walt," drawled the Kid, in a voice which showed no sympathy. "I hope he's not planted close to drinking water or growing things. You mean Hickey come here looking for pappy?"

"*Sí!*" admitted the woman. "I couldn't hardly believe it myself. That high-quality gal sure has something."

"That was Belle Boyd, the Rebel Spy," the Kid told her. "What's going on, Rosey gal?"

"Ramon and the Bully's after your pappy and the gal. From what they've said, there'll be more folks looking. So they're working in cahoots and figure to split the money between 'em."

"So word's got out," the Kid breathed.

"Three Yankee steam launches've gone up river passing it," Rosita replied. "Big Sam said to tell you he's swung off to the south."

"Peraro and old Bully's got fellers along who can read sign

real good," the Kid remarked. "I'd's soon not have 'em dogging my tracks when I go after pappy."

"You want for me to put something in their *tequila?*" Rosita inquired.

"Does that firewater need anything in it?" countered the Kid, and grinned at the pungent, obscene defense of the *posada's* liquor. Then he went on, "Nope. Don't you chance it, Rosey. I'll tend to things myself."

All too well the Kid knew Peraro's and Segan's vindictive nature. Let either of them feel the slightest breath of suspicion and no amount of potential family backing could save Rosita. So the youngster intended, if possible, to halt the pursuit in a manner that would leave her free from blame.

"I'll do anything I can, Lon," Rosita promised.

"I know that—you never did have a lick of good sense. Got some Ysabel blood in you, most likely. Only I got me a right sneaky, treacherous notion. Where're their hosses?"

"In the corral, all except Peraro's black stallion."

"That figures. He allus keeps it in a stable if he can."

"And with that Yaqui of his standing guard on it," Rosita warned. "I could send something out—"

"Damned if I'll chance eating here again," grinned the Kid, "way you're so set on slipping something into the stuff. Nope, Rosey. Happen you want to help, just hint around that Ramon might have some more fellers out 'n' about."

"You'll never get the black!" Rosita began.

"Likely not," the Kid agreed, although the time would come when he had to steal Peraro's well-guarded favorite horse.* But Bully's *bayo-coyote's* in the corral and not guarded. Ole Bully sets a heap o' store by that hoss."

"It's a good hoss," Rosita answered.

"Yeah," the Kid replied. "And wouldn't he be all riled up happen it's gone comes morning?"

"It's a big chance, Cabrito."

"Yes'm. A real big chance."

* Told in *The Texan.*

Silence fell, and Rosita realized that the Kid had gone. Sucking in a deep breath, she rose from the backhouse seat, shook down her skirts, and returned to the *posada*.

Although he went back to his horse, the Kid did not intend to make a move straight away. There would be no point in going on, for he needed daylight to find his father's and Belle's tracks. More important, he must attempt to prevent the two gangs from following them. Trying to do so in an open fight offered too little chance of success to be contemplated. So he planned another way. If one of the gangs found some of its horses missing, the blame would fall on its rivals.

Taking Peraro's horse from the stable would be difficult. So, despite his desire to attempt the feat, he decided against trying. Down in the corral stood an easier mark. Unless his boyhood training had left him—and he knew it had not—he should be able to achieve his ends.

Satisfied, he off-saddled the white and allowed it to roll on the grass while making his own preparations to catch some rest.

Like Belle, the Kid could wake at any time he set himself to. Sitting up, he looked around, darted a glance at the sky, and estimated how long he had slept. Then he rose and moved to where he could see the *posada*. No lights showed at any of the windows, although a lantern still glowed in the stable. To one side the white stallion lay sleeping, but it woke and raised its head as he walked back to his saddle.

"Settle down again, ole hoss," the Kid said quietly, unfastening the coiled rope from the saddlehorn. "I won't be needin' you for a spell yet."

Leaving the horse still resting, the youngster made his way through the darkness toward the *posada*. Although not really needing one, he used the light from the stables as a guide and directed his silent feet toward the corral. Eyes and ears worked constantly to catch any slight warning of danger as the Kid drew closer to his destination. Probably as a sign of their trust and faith in each other, neither gang appeared to have a man guarding the horses in the corral. Peraro could continue to do so with his black stallion, for he always did, even in the safety of his hideout.

Raiding—horse-stealing—always rated high in the ways a Comanche could gain honor, and boys received a very thorough training in all aspects of the art. So the Kid possessed all the knowledge he would need to carry out his scheme. In his hand he held his rope, a most useful extension of his will when properly used. On reaching the downwind side of the corral, he paused to study the situation and decide which horses he wanted to steal. For his idea to work out properly, he must take horses belonging only to Bully Segan's gang.

Selecting the required animals, even in darkness, proved easy to a man of the Kid's encyclopedic equine knowledge. Horses being gregarious by nature, they tended to bunch with those of their kind to which they were most familiar. So the Kid could make out three well-defined groups in the corral. Even without being able to point directly at Segan's big *bayo-coyote* stallion, he quickly learned which of the groups belonged to the white men. Easing around so that the wind bore his scent into the corral, he watched the horses' reactions. Mexican animals gave signs of restlessness at catching a white man's scent; not as much as Indian ponies would, but sufficient for the Kid's needs. With the ownership of the groups established, the rest was easy. Even before he withdrew downwind, he had located the Segan's highly prized mount.

Before entering the corral, the Kid took out his knife and slit the rope into three twenty-foot lengths. Normally an Indian on a raiding mission took along the ropes ready prepared, but the Kid had not expected the need to arise. However, a small matter like that created little difficulty. Swiftly he made running nooses on two of the pieces, the original honda remaining to be used on the third. With all ready, he approached the corral gate openly. A low hissing whistle left his lips, alerting the horses to his presence without disturbing them. Fortunately even Rosita O'Malley's stock saw enough arrivals in the darkness not to take fright at his approach, and the gangs' mounts regarded such behavior as natural.

Carefully the Kid eased out the gate bars, lowering the ends he held to the ground. A quick glance around told him his presence still remained unsuspected, and he entered the corral. Keeping up the soothing hissing, he moved among the horses. If any of them showed signs of restlessness, he stopped like a statue until the animal quietened down once more. At last he reached the *bayo-coyote,* and it faced him with alert but not frightened attention. Using the same unhurried, calm manner that had covered his every movement since entering the corral, the Kid raised the rope and slipped its honda-formed loop over the horse's head. Giving a snort, the *bayo-coyote* tossed its head. If the Kid had so much as flinched, the stallion might have attacked; but he stood like a statue and continued the low, comforting whistle. Then the noose drew tight, and the worst danger passed. Feeling the familiar touch of a rope, the horse stood fast and awaited the next command. Before attempting anything further, the Kid drew gently but insistently on the rope. As the sleek head lowered, he blew into its nostrils. Back in the days when the Comanche obtained the first of the "god-dogs" from the Spanish explorers, it had been learned that breathing into a horse's nostrils quietened it and rendered it amenable to orders. Nor did the *bayo-coyote* prove any exception, having received the treatment many times since its capture and training. Gently and without fuss, the Kid won the horse's confidence and dominated its will.

Gathering two more of the horses belonging to Segan's gang took less time and presented no problems. As its owner ran the gang, so the *bayo-coyote* led their mounts. Seeing it accept the newcomer, the others stood steady enough. Leading his three captives, the Kid walked slowly around the corral and through the gate. If anybody had been watching, it seemed that the trio of horses did no more than move aimlessly. Only while passing through the gate could the difference be seen. All the rest of the Segan gang's horses followed, but he turned them back at the gate. Three would be enough for his plan, and to handle more added noise and risk. Knotting the three lead ropes together, he left his captives standing while he replaced the corral gates.

"Grandpappy Long Walker'd be proud of me," the Kid grinned as he reached for the knotted lead ropes. "Sure wish I'd a pair o' wored-out ole moccasins along—naw, that'd give the whole snap away for sure."

Often a successful Comanche raider would leave a sign of his presence to mock the people he robbed. A favorite trick was to leave behind an ancient pair of moccasins. Then when the owners discovered their loss they read the message that the raider no longer needed his old footwear as he could ride off in comfort on the stolen horses.

Much as the Kid wished he could play the old ending to his raid, he knew it would be impossible and impracticable. He did not have a pair of old moccasins along. Even if he had, using them in such a manner might ruin his scheme. Seeing the old Comanche sign might point out an alternative remover of the horses to Segan. The Kid's connection with that particular Indian tribe being well known, his activities could be understood and the desired trouble between the gangs averted.

So, regretfully putting aside the thought, he led the horses around the outside of the corral and, on the opposite side to the stables, off toward where his white stallion waited. Picketing them securely out of sight of the corral, he returned to his interrupted sleep. By the first light of dawn he woke, packed his gear, saddled the white, and returned to a position from which he could watch the cantina.

Soon after the Kid took his place, a couple of Segan's men walked from the building and in the direction of the corral. Then the others came out, the gang leaders still apparently on the best of terms even if their men showed the same veiled hostility. Reaching the corral, the first pair came to a halt, staring at the horses.

"Now cut for sign, you stupid yahoos!" breathed the Kid.

Almost as if they heard him, the men directed their eyes to the ground and started around the corral. At last they halted, pointing down. Without attempting to follow the tracks further, they turned and dashed back the way they came.

"Bully!" one of them yelled. "Your hoss's gone. And two more."

"Gone!" Segan bellowed and started toward the corral.

Standing at the door of the cantina to see her guests depart, Rosita decided to add her touch to the Kid's plan.

"Hey, Ramon," she called in Spanish. "I've sent Yaqui his breakfast to the stable. What an appetite. He eats enough for two."

Harmless enough sounding words, but sufficient to raise unpleasant thoughts in Segan's head. Suspicious by nature, he read what Rosita hoped he would in her words. There had been other hints during the previous night that Peraro might have more than the one man outside the *posada*. While accepting that Yaqui was standing guard on the black stallion, in the interests of retaining Peraro's good will until after relieving the Ysabels of the money, Segan drew sinister conclusions from Rosita's innocent statement.

Three of Segan's gang would be without horses, even if he took one of their mounts for himself. He did not wish to help bushwhack the Ysabels unless sure that he had enough men at his back to protect his interests.

Never known for his tact, but famous as a hater of gringos, Peraro's second in command, Perez, could not resist injecting a mocking comment.

"You lose something, *Matón?*" he asked, with a grin at his companions.

"You're damned right I lost something!" Segan answered, swinging around to face the Mexicans. "Where are they, Peraro?"

"*Matón*, Bully, *amigo,*" Peraro replied. "I don't know what you mean."

However, he stood tense, balancing lightly on the balls of his feet. One night's drinking could not wipe away decades of antipathy caused by racial differences and working in active competition. No more than a precaution on Peraro's part, it increased Segan's suspicions and anger.

Quickly Rosita drew the cantina door closed. Not suspicious

in itself. Born and raised on the border, she could read the signs. At the first hint of trouble, even without prior knowledge of its coming, she would have acted in the same manner.

"Where's my hoss?" Segan demanded. "Where the hell did your son of a bitch take it to?"

"I'm not sure that I like that question, *hombre!*" Peraro answered, with the silky deadliness of a highborn Spanish fighting man. "If you can't keep hold of your horses, I am not to blame."

"Keep 'em!" Segan bellowed. "I'll damned soon get 'em back."

Despite having an old Walker Colt hanging in his holster, Segan snatched the long-bladed knife from its sheath and sprang at Peraro. Moving even faster, the Mexican also fanned out his shorter but no less deadly blade. With the fluid grace of a matador avoiding the charge of a bull, Peraro sidestepped Segan's rush. As the heavy copy of a James Black bowie lashed harmlessly by him, the Mexican delivered a ripping thrust to the attacker's body. Letting out a croaking cry of agony, Segan staggered by Peraro, dropped his knife, clawed at his belly, and crashed to his knees at the porch.

"You never should've tried a knife, Bully," the Kid commented, watching with satisfaction.

One of Segan's men showed a better grasp of the situation than his boss. Whipping the revolver from his belt, he fired. The bullet caught Peraro in the shoulder, spinning him around and tumbling him to the ground. Out came more guns, and men dashed for cover to continue the fight.

Satisfied that everything in his scheme was going as he wanted, the Kid returned to his horses. With both leaders incapacitated, the Ysabels and Belle Boyd need not fear pursuit from either gang. Finding his father's tracks took only a short time. Using his newly acquired horses, the Kid could push on at a better pace. From what Rosita had told him and he had seen at the *posada,* the sooner they joined forces the better.

11

THEY'LL PAY TO GET
HER BACK

Due to nursing his throbbing jaw and thinking what he would
do to Amy-Jo when he laid hands on her, Hickey rode through
the darkness without his usual caution. Nor did the men with
him show greater alertness, being concerned with their own
sufferings. Before they could stop themselves or realize the danger, the trio found themselves covered by the guns of three
horsemen who loomed out of the bushes.

For a moment panic filled Hickey, then he recognized the
stocky shape on the nearest horse.

"Howdy, Charlie," he greeted. "You headed for Rosita
O'Malley's?"

"Maybe," Charlie Kraus replied, holstering his Colt. "You
been there?"

"Sure. We got your word and figured Big Sam'd likely call in
to see Rosey. He was there all right."

"*You* went up against Sam Ysabel?" Kraus asked, his voice
showing how he felt on the matter.

"Sure, but him and some of his boys laid for us and whomped us good," Hickey answered.

"What is it, Mr. Kraus?" asked a woman's voice, and Eve rode forward from where she and Ffauldes had been told to wait until the approaching riders were identified. "Has he seen Ysabel and Boyd?"

"Sure," Kraus replied. "At Rosey O'Malley's place."

"They ain't there now, ma'am," Hickey put in, sensing the chance of making a little money out of the disastrous affair.

"Who's this, Mr. Kraus?" Eve inquired.

"Name's Hickey. He tried to get that money."

"Tried?"

"That'd be his best, ma'am. What happened, Hickey?"

"Big Sam was waiting for us. Nigh on bust my jaw, beat Tetch here about the head something evil, and done for poor ole Lone Tom. Rosey lay a skillet on Mick's face, and when we come to, Big Sam and that high-quality gal'd lit out."

"Where?" Eve demanded. "Along the river?"

"Down south, way Rosey told it," Hickey replied.

"She told *you* that?" Kraus growled.

"Naw. I heard her telling it to Ramon Peraro and Bully Segan."

"Peraro and Segan, huh?"

"Who are they, Mr. Kraus?" Eve put in.

"Just about the meanest, most ornery pair of killers on the Rio Grande," he explained. "Fact being, you'd be hard put to pair 'em anywheres short of hell."

"Then it wouldn't be advisable for us to go to this woman and question her about Ysabel?" Eve said.

"Ma'am," Kraus replied, "it wouldn't be advisable even without them two there. Where Ysabel's concerned, Rosey O'Malley wouldn't tell you the time of day. And with Peraro 'n' the Bully both there, it'd be plumb suicide." Then a thought struck him and he glared at Hickey. "How much did you tell Big Sam?"

"Nothing!" the man yelped. "Warn't much talkin' done

when we met up, and time I'd got round to feelin' like it again, he'd pulled out."

"Where's Amy-Jo?" Kraus growled.

"She—she pulled out," Hickey admitted.

"Afore you come round?"

"Yeah. And when I lay hands on her, I'll make her wish she'd never learned to talk!"

"So she told Big Sam how you got on to him?"

"She told him," agreed Hickey. "You can't blame her, Charlie. Big Sam's got mighty fetching ways when he gets that way inclined."

"That means Ysabel and Boyd know what we've done," Eve remarked. "Here, take this ten dollars and ride!"

Grabbing the money, Hickey gabbled his thanks while putting the spurs to his horse. Followed by his men, he set off through the darkness at a gallop.

"That stupid—!" Kraus began. "A bullet'd been more his needings."

Satisfied that there would be no danger, Ffauldes rode up to assert himself. He had heard everything said and felt he should give the others the benefit of his superior ability.

"So they've left the river trail," he began.

"Maybe," Kraus replied. "You can't be sure of anything with Sam Ysabel and less with the Kid."

"Your partner stayed in Matamoros to deal with the Kid," Ffauldes pointed out. "He took our money to hire extra help to do it."

"Staying there's one thing, getting help's easy," Kraus grunted. "Stopping the Kid's another again. It's been tried afore—he's still around even if the folks who tried it ain't."

"Damn it! Your partner—"

"Joe'll do the best he can, mister," Kraus interrupted. "Right now it's Big Sam, not the Kid, I'm thinking about."

"We can pick up their trail at the *posada,*" Ffauldes started.

"And while we're followin' it slow, which's the only way it'll be followed, Big Sam and the gal'll be at the other end makin' more tracks," Kraus told him. "Top of that, *mister,* Bully Segan and Ramon Peraro ain't gonna take kind to more folk trailin' along to share the money."

"They'd object to us going along?" Eve asked.

"They'd object to each other goin' along, happen one of 'em's got enough men to do it," Kraus replied. "We don't have near enough men to tangle with 'em."

"What do you think Ysabel will do?" Eve said, after a moment's thought.

"I dunno," Kraus admitted. "He'll know that by now every robbin' son of a bitch along the river's heard, or enough of 'em, and'll be huntin' for him. I'd say he'll keep to the south, at least until he gets near Nava. You wanna try huntin' for him?"

"No," Eve decided. "We'll go up the river. I want to contact the steam-launch flotilla, and if Ysabel gets through, I'll be there ready to send warning to our garrisons in New Mexico."

Before Ffauldes could make another comment, Kraus gave the signal to start moving. Clearly the stocky man had decided who was running the affair and accepted Eve's suggestions.

There had been a heated scene in Matamoros when Eve laid her plans for the journey and announced that she would take one man along. That was a simple precaution, for she doubted if Kraus would be reliable if things went wrong. Much to her annoyance, Ffauldes had pulled rank and insisted that he be the one to accompany her. That she agreed had been less a tribute to his capabilities than the desire to keep him under her eyes. The French agreed to allow the *Waterbury* into Matamoros for the purpose of repairing her damaged hull. Expecting the Confederate agents to make a further attempt, Eve gave strict instructions to the Yankee detachment for the ship's protection. So she gave in to Ffauldes's demands, taking him with her to prevent his interference or ruination of her arrangements.

Patriotism did not lie behind Ffauldes's insistence, nor devotion to duty. Knowing the state of affairs in the United States, he could imagine the acclaim that would come to the man who ruined the South's desperate final bid. With the war almost over, that man could expect recognition that would still be fresh in the public's memory when the handing out of rewards

commenced. So he joined Eve's party and promised himself
that he alone would garner the credit. However, he soon
learned that Eve commanded the expedition. All through the
first day's journey Kraus made that plain.

Bypassing Rosita O'Malley's *posada* shortly before the Kid
arrived, they pushed on a further two miles and made camp.
Next morning, following Eve's orders, they continued to go
west along the banks of the river. They traveled fast, changing
horses as needed. Visiting various gathering places for the crim-
inal element, Kraus reported on the lack of men present. Twice
the party were halted and challenged by armed gangs, to be let
pass after establishing their identity. On one occasion they
fought off a bunch of Mexicans who objected to another party
apparently on the trail of Ysabel and the money. At Nuevo
Laredo, Kraus went into town with one of his men while Eve
and the remainder stayed outside. He returned with news that
both the French and Juaristas were interested in the gold, adding more searchers for Ysabel and the Rebel Spy.

At noon on the day after passing Nuevo Laredo, the party
met up with the launch flotilla and its commanding officer reported on his activities. He had taken his command along the
river as far as Piedras Negras, returning without the Texas
citizens of Eagle Pass learning of their presence. Telling the
officer of her plans, Eve arranged for him to patrol between
Piedras Negras and Nuevo Laredo. Then, if they received word
about Ysabel and Belle Boyd reaching Klatwitter, it could be
acted upon without waste of time.

While Eve was conversing with the U.S. Navy lieutenant, she
saw Kraus talking to Golly. The two men stood clear of the
others and she noticed that Golly pointed across to the Texas
bank of the river. When questioned, Kraus said that he and
Golly had discussed the chances of meeting with Texan opposition.

Leaving the flotilla to complete taking on wood for fuel, the
party continued its journey. The day went by without incident;
so did the next until the late afternoon. By that time they had
come close to the town of Nava, although still sticking to the

river. As usual Kraus had men ahead as scouts. With the proximity of the danger area, he used two instead of the usual one scout and they returned in some haste. Then followed a conversation in Spanish so rapid that neither Eve nor Ffauldes could follow it. Eve caught one word, *Danvila,* probably because it came several times and was spoken with some feeling.

"What's wrong, Mr. Kraus?" she asked.

"We've got to turn back," he replied. "There's a big bunch of Juaristas up ahead."

"We've no quarrel with them," Eve stated. "And I've a letter from our consul in Matamoros explaining our presence."

"Maybe you won't get time to show it," Kraus pointed out.

"Very well. We'll go and make camp by the river until the flotilla comes by," Eve decided. "With two cannon and a Gatling gun at our backs, they'll listen."

A point with which Kraus could not argue. In fact he seemed more cheerful at being reminded of the flotilla's assault armament. As she had never seen one, Amy-Jo had failed to identify the six-barreled, .58-caliber Gatling gun the lieutenant's launch carried in place of the usual 12-pounder boat howitzer. Such weapons, especially the Gatling gun, would impress the Juaristas and make them amenable to discussion.

Raising no more objections, Kraus led the way farther upstream until finding a suitable campsite. Tired from the hard, long journey, Eve removed her boots and rolled fully dressed into her blankets. She fell asleep almost immediately and deeply. Just how deeply she discovered on waking.

The morning sun hung just above the horizon as she sat up and reached to where her boots should be. Then her sleep-slowed mind registered that something must be wrong. She heard Mexican voices, which did not in itself surprise her, for few of Kraus's men spoke English. What came as a surprise was the high-pitched tones of women mingled with the voices of the men. At the same moment she became aware that her boots no longer stood by the bed.

Jerking upright, Eve stared around her. There was no sign of Kraus and his men. Instead, half a dozen well-armed, hard-faced men in *vaquero* dress and two pretty young women stood around the camp. One of the women was drawing on Eve's boots, while the other petulantly watched a man up-ending Eve's saddlebags.

"If you look for Charlie, *señorita,*" said the tallest of the men, walking toward Eve. "He's gone."

"Who are you?" she demanded, glancing to where Ffauldes was sitting covered by one of the newcomers' rifles.

"Joaquim Sandos, *señorita,*" the man replied. "Didn't Charlie speak about me, or tell you his fellers saw Pancho there yesterday and know we come looking for him?"

"He didn't. Why do you want to see him?"

"He not tell you much, *señorita.* Didn't he say how I'm Cosme Danvila's *segundo?*" Sandos asked. "Him and Cosme, they not good friends since Charlie shoot Cosme's brother and leave his sister with a little *niño.* I never think to see Charlie this far west. Unless he hear that Cosme across the river in Texas on—business."

"I see," Eve said quietly.

Which she did. Clearly Kraus had only accompanied her that far because Golly had brought him word of his enemy's absence. She remembered the pointing across the river when they met the flotilla. Then Kraus must have learned the previous afternoon that not all Danvila's band had gone on the raid. The story about a Juarista force had been fabricated as an excuse to turn back. Probably Kraus was hoping for the arrival of the flotilla. When it did not come, or possibly because he had learned that Sandos's party was drawing near, Kraus slipped away with his men. Eve could even understand why he had deserted her. Neither she nor Ffauldes could handle horses quietly in the dark, or stand up to a hard, fast flight. So, to Kraus's practical way of thinking, leaving them behind offered the only solution.

"Maybe Charlie leave her as a presen' for Cosme," suggested the man searching Eve's belongings.

"No. He was guiding me to El Paso," Eve answered. "My husband is in the army there."

"You not a *Tejano, señorita,* and you don't wear a wedding ring," Sandos pointed out. "And there're no soldiers at El Paso."

"She's an important member of the United States government," Ffauldes put in. "So am I. Show them that letter from the consul, Miss Coniston."

"Can I?" Eve inquired and, receiving Sandos's nod, took the letter from the pocket of her divided skirt.

However, if the way Sandos examined the sheet of paper was anything to go by, he could not read the consul's request that Eve be given free passage through to El Paso.

"You got 'nother pair of boots, *señorita?*" Sandos asked, thrusting the paper into his pocket. "Rosa and Juanita never had any before and Rosa wants a pair."

"Look, mister!" Ffauldes put in, standing up and showing that he was not wearing a gun. "She's real important, but I'm not."

"Shut your mouth!" Eve snapped, and then smiled at Sandos. "I'm not important at all."

"Is a pity if you're not, *señorita.* If you not Charlie's *amante,* sweetheart you call him, maybe somebody pay good to get you back."

"You can bet they'll pay to get her back!" Ffauldes agreed eagerly. "There're three small steamboats on the river. If you let me go to them, they'll take me to Matamoros and I'll bring you the money."

"I'll just bet you will!" Eve spat out.

"The *señorita* she don' trust you, *hombre,*" Sandos remarked.

"What have I to lose?" Ffauldes spat back. "Let me go to the boats and I'll arrange everything."

"Go get on your horse, *señor,*" Sandos ordered.

Without as much as a glance at Eve, Ffauldes started to obey. Sandos nodded as Ffauldes walked toward the two horses left by Kraus. Even as Eve opened her mouth to scream a warning, two rifles cracked. Lead ripped into Ffauldes's back and he sprawled facedown on the ground. Letting her breath out in a gasp, Eve tried to go toward the stricken man.

"I think he wouldn't've come back, *señorita*," Sandos remarked, stopping her. "He look like my uncle Sebastian, and he one big liar. Will anybody pay to get you back?"

For a moment Eve did not reply. Then she realized that her only chance of staying alive would be to answer in the affirmative. Resistance would be futile, so she decided to go along with what might offer her a hope of escape.

"Yes. They'll pay to get me back. Or the authorities over the border will give you money for me. I'm a United States agent. If you look for the boats, they'll go at top speed to Brownsville for the money."

"You a spy for the *Estados Unidos*, heh?"

"Yes."

"I think you tell the truth this time. But it for Cosme to say what we do with you."

"Is Señor Danvila hunting for Sam Ysabel?" Eve inquired, suddenly realizing that Sandos had not mentioned the matter.

"Nobody goes hunting for Big Sam, *señorita*," Sandos replied. "Not if they want to stay alive."

"Even if he has fifteen thousand dollars in gold with him?"

"You make the joke with Sandos, no?"

"I'm not joking, *señor*. Ysabel and the Rebel Spy, a girl, are taking the gold to the French general at Nava."

"Maybe they won't get it there," Sandos grinned.

"Why don't you go and find them?" Eve asked.

"With six men?" Sandos scoffed, and spoke to his companions.

Eve judged that he was telling them the news and all seemed to find the latter part highly amusing.

"If you don't believe me, send one of your men along the river, to find the boats," Eve said. "They will tell him, the sailors. Or he could go to Pasear Hennessey's cantina. Kraus's man, Golly, came up river with the boats to tell everybody about Big Sam and the money."

"Nobody from Charlie Kraus would come near us, *señorita*,"

Sandos replied. "We take you to our camp and I send for Cosme. He say what we do."

They mounted Eve on the sorriest of their horses when ready to move out, one that looked incapable of outrunning a turtle in its swaybacked, gaunt-ribbed condition. Gathering up all they wanted and hiding Ffauldes's stripped body in the bushes, the men and girls surrounded Eve and rode off. Instead of sticking to the river's bank, they rode parallel to it but some distance away. However, the country was open enough for Eve to see the water and she scanned it eagerly in the hope of seeing the flotilla.

Manned by veterans of the Mississippi Squadron, who carried Navy Colts, cutlasses, and Spencer carbines in addition to the cannons and Gatling gun, the three launches held the means of her escape. Although sailors, the crews knew plenty about land fighting and, if they heard of her capture, might contrive a rescue.

"Look!" one of the men said, pointing toward the river.

The three launches came into sight, going upstream. Instantly the Mexicans gathered closer about Eve and a knife's point pricked against her ribs. Wisely she kept quiet and the launches went by without knowing of her presence. Then Sandos grinned at her.

"You behave good, *señorita,* and I think maybe you tell the truth."

Riding on, the Mexicans kept a watch behind them, but the launches did not return. The river curved through a valley at that point, the Texas shore rising plainly on the other side. Down below Eve, thick clumps of bushes grew down to the water's edge, interspersed with open patches of sandy beach that would be bays and backwaters in time of flood. Ahead, the country became more open than ever and the bushes ended on a large patch of open beach.

A horse whinnied from among the bushes, the sound chopping off as if stopped in some way. Immediately the party came to a halt. An order from Santos sent three of the men riding cautiously toward the source of the sound, and the other three held rifles ready for use. Not that Eve saw a chance to escape, for the two girls flanked her holding knives ready for use.

Suddenly a rider burst into view, racing down the slope toward the river. Eve bit down a startled exclamation at the sight. Dressed in male clothing, with black hair cropped boyishly short, the rider was without doubt a woman. Unless Eve missed her guess, it was *the* woman, the Rebel Spy.

Flame ripped from one of the advancing trio's rifle and the fleeing woman's horse went down, pitching her from its saddle. She landed sprawling on the soft sand, and before she had recovered, the three men advanced, surrounding her. Bending down, one of the three pulled the Dance Brothers revolver from her holster. Then he waved his companions to join him and the woman sat up.

Eve sucked in a deep breath as she rode with the others down the slope. It seemed that the Rebel Spy had fallen into the Mexican *bandidos'* hands. The problem facing Eve was what to do about it.

12
THE FORT IS UNDER ATTACK

"Lon's coming, Miss Belle," said Sam Ysabel, after making one of his periodic searches of their backtrail.

Relief lay under the laconic tone and Belle mirrored the feeling. Almost three days had gone by since they left the O'Malley *posada*. After the first day, Ysabel clearly expected the Kid to arrive by the hour. Although he never mentioned it, the girl guessed that he felt a growing concern for his son's safety as the time went by.

Turning in her saddle, the girl looked back and saw only small, indistinct specks on the horizon. However, she had seen enough of Ysabel to know that he would not make a mistake.

"There's more than one horse," she said after a moment.

"Mebbe Lon borrowed some from Rosey to ride relay," Ysabel replied. "Only he'd've been along sooner if he had. He's coming fast now."

"We'd best wait for him, then," Belle suggested.

Nodding, Ysabel led the way to a clump of bushes. By the

time they had halted in concealment, the blobs had come close enough for Belle to make out definite shapes. Ysabel saw far more. Enough to bring a low-voiced exclamation from his lips.

"Well I'm damned!"

"That's more than likely," said Belle, smiling, having grown to like and respect the big man during their journey. While he might lack many of the social graces, at no time had he acted in any but a proper manner toward her. "But why the sudden realization?"

"If the boy ain't wide-looped Bully Segan's *bayo-coyote* hoss, I'll be a Tejas Injun's squaw."

"I don't know the gentleman—not that I suppose he is a gentleman—but I'll take your word that it is his horse."

"Bully won't take happy to losing it," Ysabel drawled. "That means—"

Allowing the words to trail off, the big man made another of his careful searches of the surrounding country. Then he turned his attention to his son. No longer did the white stallion have black patches on its coat. The *bayo-coyote* and the third horse showed signs of hard travel and use.

"Howdy, boy," Ysabel greeted as his son rode up.

"Howdy, *ap',* " the Kid replied, using the Comanche term for father. "Howdy, Miss Belle. Got me some antelope steaks for supper. Reckon we'd best be moving on."

"How about the horses, Lon?" Belle asked.

"Hosses? Which hosses?" the Kid said innocently. "Oh, *them* hosses. I just happened on 'em."

"The Bully likely to be raising a fuss about you 'happening' on to his *bayo-coyote* there?" Ysabel growled.

"I'd say 'no' to that," drawled the Kid, eyes darting around him as he spoke. "Seems he got to blaming Ramon Peraro for the hoss goin' missin'. Damned if he didn't try to do the blamin' with a knife."

"Well, doggie!" Ysabel ejaculated. "If that don't beat all. So ole Bully won't be comin' along?"

"Nor Ramon neither," the Kid confirmed. "One of Bully's boys had a mite more sense and started throwin' lead. I don't reckon Ramon'll be riding for a spell. I'd've been along sooner, only a bunch of Juaristas got after me and I led 'em around for a spell afore losing 'em."

Which did not tell the entire story. Coming across the Juaristas without their knowledge, the Kid heard enough to know they hunted for his father and Belle. So he washed the stain from the white's coat and allowed himself to be seen from a distance. Then he kept out of sight but left tracks for the men to follow. When sure they would be unable to catch up to his father, he lost his pursuers and resumed his journey. Heading south, he located his father's and Belle's tracks at last and found them. Doing so cost him one of the horses stolen from Segan's gang.

"Saw some smoke this mornin'," he went on. "Likely you couldn't. Too much for just a campfire. Figured I'd best catch up fast. Let's go."

Used as she had become to Sam Ysabel's caution, Belle could not help but notice how much more alert he seemed to be when they resumed the journey. She put it down to fears that Bully Segan, whoever he might be, was on their trail. Yet that did not explain why the Ysabels freed their buckskin saddleboots and rode with the rifles still encased but across their arms. Still pondering on their behavior, she turned to ask a question.

"Drop behind us, Miss Belle!" the Kid said urgently. "And take these hosses."

"What—?" Belle began, accepting the reins of the spare mounts and packhorse which he thrust into her hands.

"Do it, *pronto!*" Ysabel interrupted. "And whatever happens, stop back there. Don't make a move or speak unless I tell you."

Although surprised at the man's behavior, Belle obeyed. She knew they must have good reasons for their actions, so she neither asked questions nor raised snobbish points of social standing, rank, or sex.

For almost two minutes they rode on. Then, suddenly, the country before them became dotted with Indians. Squat, thick-set braves seemed to rise out of the ground, seated on their ponies and armed with a variety of weapons.

Immediately the Kid gripped his rifle at the wrist of the butt and end of barrel, raising it above his head. A moment later Ysabel repeated the gesture and Belle became aware that neither of her escorts had removed the covering from his rifle. Fighting down a desire to draw her Dance, the girl sat still and waited to see what developed.

One of the Indians, sporting a long war bonnet, raised his war lance in the same manner. Lowering it again, he took his right hand away to make a sign in the trio's direction. Taking his right hand from the rifle, the Kid held it palm downward before his chest. Then he moved his bent arm to the right in a wriggling motion.

Whatever the sign might mean, Belle could see no change in the Indians' attitude. After a moment they sent their horses leaping forward, charging down on the trio at full speed.

"Sit fast and don't touch that Dance, Miss Belle!" Ysabel growled over his shoulder and the girl guessed he was speaking with the minimum of lip movement.

The next few seconds seemed to be the longest Belle could ever remember. Nearer thundered the Indians, looking meaner than all hell and more deadly than a stampeding herd of buffalo. Then, when there appeared to be no way to avoid being ridden down, the Indians split around them and came to a halt. Belle had never seen such fine riding, although she admitted that most of the finer points were lost on her at that moment.

For a moment nobody spoke, then the war-bonnet chief let out a guttural growl of words. Listening to the Kid's reply, Belle caught only two familiar words, "Ysabel" and *"cuchilo,"* which she knew to be Spanish for knife. Her quick ears noticed that the Kid spoke more slowly than the chief—much as a Texan's speech differed from a New Englander's—but she put that down to his using a foreign language. She could not fail to notice the deprecating manner with which the Kid waved a hand in her direction, then indicated his father.

More talk followed, some laughter, and the Ysabels passed

out tobacco. Then the two parties separated. Even so, Ysabel warned the girl to remain behind, and not until a mile lay between them and the Indians did he offer an explanation for his and the Kid's behavior.

"I reckon we can get divorced now, Miss Belle," he said, halting the horse and grinning at her.

"Divorced?" she repeated. "What was that all about?"

"They're *Pahuraix,* Water Horse Comanches, on a raid. Lon saw their scout just in time for us to make things look right. These medicine boots Long Walker gave us let 'em know we belonged to the *Pehnane* band and we allowed that you was my squaw."

"And no Indian would let his squaw ride at his side, or lead the horses with her along," Belle smiled.

"Not on a trail in country like this," Ysabel agreed. "We're through 'em now, but we'd best keep going."

"It was a close call," Belle stated rather than guessed.

"Too close," Ysabel replied. "Happen we hadn't been toting these medicine boots on the rifles, they mightn't've give us time to start talking. With them, the *Pahuraix* figured they'd best see who we were afore they killed us. Lon's Long Walker's grandson: killing him'd start off a blood feud."

Listening to the quiet words, Belle found herself blessing the good fortune that had given her such able companions, and not for the first time since meeting the Ysabel family. She could realize just how dangerous the situation had been. Only the Kid's alertness and relationship to the *Pehnane* war chief had saved them.

As they rode on to the west, Ysabel explained how the Kid had used the traditional sign when the *Pahuraix* chief asked for information as to their tribe. Speaking the slow *Pehnane* dialect that had attracted Belle's attention, the Kid introduced himself as Cuchilo, grandson of Long Walker, and explained that he and his father were riding on private business, accompanied by the latter's squaw. After an exchange of information and the latest jokes, the *Pahuraix* went on their way.

Despite their belief that the *Pahuraix* had accepted their

bona fides, the Ysabels insisted that they make a camp in wooded country that night. A *tuivitsi,* young warrior, might decide to ignore the threat of a blood feud with the *Pehnane* and try to win acclaim by stealing their horses. So they settled down for the night in an area through which silent progress would be difficult.

Always a light sleeper, Belle woke in the night. She saw the Kid and his father standing by the dying embers of the fire and sat up. Turning, the Kid raised a finger to his lips.

"There's somebody out that ways, Miss Belle," he said, coming to the girl's side and pointing into the blackness.

"One of the Indians?" she whispered back.

"Nope. Too noisy and wearing boots. I'm going to take a look, see who it is. Stay put and keep your Dance handy."

With that the Kid turned and disappeared into the woods. He went in silence, flickering out of the girl's sight with his knife in hand. Joining Belle, holding a Sharps rifle, Ysabel nodded after his departing son.

"Knife's better than any gun in the dark and among the trees."

"I suppose so," Belle replied. "We must be close to Nava now?"

"Be there late tomorrow night, or before noon the day after," Ysabel replied. "Depends on who's around."

Five minutes went by, then a whistle sounded in the darkness.

"Lon?" asked Belle.

"Sure," Ysabel answered, putting down his rifle at her side. "Wait here."

Rising, Belle watched Ysabel walk away. In a short time he returned, helping his son to carry a man in uniform. Belle tossed a few sticks onto the fire and its glow allowed them to study the newcomer.

"A French Huzzar," Belle said as the Ysabels lay the man by the fire. "He's been shot!"

"Late this afternoon, I'd say," Ysabel replied. "Lord knows how he's come this far."

"Maybe saw the fire and come toward it," the Kid went on as Belle ran forward to kneel at the man's side. "He's near on bled white and just about gone."

Opening his eyes, the Huzzar stared vacantly around for a moment. Then a flicker of realization showed in them and he began to speak haltingly. Only by bending forward could Belle catch the words. At first he talked sensibly, then began to ramble. His hand clutched the girl's arm, tightened, and went loose.

"He's done," Ysabel said quietly.

"Yes," Belle replied.

"What'd he say?" asked the Kid.

"That the fort is under attack by a large force of Juaristas armed with cannon," the girl told her companions. "Klatwitter sent two of them to fetch help, but the Mexicans killed his companion and wounded him before his horse outran them. He doesn't think they can hold out."

For a moment neither the Kid nor his father spoke. Then the youngster let out a low-growled curse.

"That's just about all we need."

"Have the Juaristas any cannon?" Belle inquired.

"The Mexican army has, and a whole slew of 'em are fighting for Juarez," Ysabel replied.

"Can they take Klatwitter?" the girl asked.

"That fort at Nava was built to stand off Injuns, not soldiers with cannon," Ysabel answered. "But if Klatwitter's got a thousand men and guns of his own he just might do it."

"Trouble being we just can't go riding up there to see him," the Kid put in.

"That's for sure," Ysabel agreed.

"The Juaristas might let us through if they knew why we wanted to see Klatwitter," Belle remarked.

"Could be," Ysabel said. "Thing being, can we trust the Juaristas? Some of 'em we know and're honest as they come. Others run Peraro and Bully Segan close for ornery meanness. Fifteen thousand dollars in gold'd come in useful to Juarez."

"You don't think we'd be advised to take it with us?"

"I reckon we'd be plumb foolish to take it," Ysabel corrected. "Look, Miss Belle, what I'd say is this. We've got a hideaway down by the river; nobody's found it yet. Let's cache the money there. Then Lon and me'll make a fast ride to Nava and see what's doing."

"We'll go Injun-style, ma'am," the Kid went on. "If there's somebody we can trust with the Juaristas, we'll talk to him. Then, if they'll agree, we'll come back to fetch you."

"That would be best," Belle admitted. "My orders are that this money must not fall into the wrong hands."

"That's how we play it then," Ysabel stated. "We'll take this feller into the woods and leave him. There's no way we can bury him. Comes morning, we'll head for the river."

"Will it be safe?" Belle asked.

"Nowhere's safe for us right now," Ysabel replied grimly. "Only where we're headed's in Cosme Danvila's neck of the woods. Him and Charlie Kraus hate each other like the devil hates holy water. I don't figure Golly'd pass the word about us to Danvila. We'll have to chance it and ride careful."

Dawn found them riding in a northwesterly direction. They traveled fast, but with caution, and saw nobody all day. Toward evening they approached the Rio Grande and Ysabel called a halt while the Kid went ahead as scout. On his return, the youngster said that their hideout remained undetected. So the party rode on once more.

Coming to a valley through which the river curved, Sam Ysabel led the way downward. They watered their horses on a wide sandbank and the Kid used a leafy branch to wipe out their tracks. Taking the horses into the thick bushes that grew close to the sandbar, Ysabel ordered that they be picketed. Then he led the girl on foot through the bushes to where a section of the valley side fell in a cliff. Still Belle could see no sign of their destination. Thrusting through some bushes, Ysabel brought the girl to the concealed mouth of a cave. Small the entrance might be, but beyond it lay a large, roomy cavern. Striking a match on the seat of his pants, Ysabel located and lit a lantern.

Looking around her in the improved light given by the lantern, Belle saw a birch-bark canoe and several familiar-looking kegs in the cave.

"We helped Rip Ford raid the Yankees and he gave us those kegs of powder," Ysabel explained. "We sent Mig and some of the boys up here with 'em to be took over to Long Walker. He's keeping the peace with the white folks and Rip figured a present was called for."

Studying the powder and canoe, Belle formed an idea. The safety of the money seemed assured, but she wished to make certain that it would not fall into the wrong hands.

"Is the canoe safe?" she asked, taking the paddle from inside it.

"Why, sure," Ysabel replied. "Feller who taught me to make 'em learned from the Blackfeet and Sioux up north."

"Then we could take the money across the river in it?"

"Sure. But it's as safe here as any place."

"I thought that we might put it in the canoe, launched ready, and take it across the river if the Juaristas should refuse to let us see Klatwitter and come after it."

"Might be best, *ap',*" the Kid remarked. "One thing's for sure. If we get it across, nobody'll follow us."

"Is the current so fast?" Belle asked.

"Nope. The bottom's quicksand once you get out a ways," drawled the Kid. "Trouble being they might get to us afore we got the boat out."

"I've thought of that," Belle said. "If we could put the money into two or three of these powder kegs and load them into the boat, we could push it off and blow the lot up rather than let it fall into the wrong hands."

"That's smart figuring, Miss Belle," Ysabel told her. "We can do it easy enough."

By that time the night had come down and so they could not launch the canoe. However, they prepared three kegs, emptying out sufficient powder from each to take the money. At dawn they moved the canoe to the river, carried down and loaded the three kegs aboard. Shoving the canoe upstream, to where the bushes grew down to the water's edge, Ysabel fastened it to the bank. Then he and his son cut branches and draped them in position to hide the canoe.

"She'll hold there, Miss Belle," Ysabel finally told the girl. "If you have to get her out fast, yank on that rope and the knot'll slip. Then push her out into the river and use the paddle to go across."

"It's a pity we haven't any fuse or slow match along," Belle remarked, walking back off the sandbar with Ysabel while the Kid removed all signs of their presence. "Then if the worst comes to the worst, we could blow up the powder."

"Should it come to that," Ysabel replied, "a bullet into one of the kegs'll do just as good as a fuse."

"It sure will," agreed the Kid, standing surveying his work. "Touch off that powder and the money's gone."

"I hope it doesn't come to that," Belle said sincerely.

If it did, as they all knew, the mission would be a failure and the South's last hope was gone.

13
WORK TOGETHER—OR DIE

After the Ysabels left, Belle settled down. Wanting to travel fast, the men took all but Belle's mount and the packhorse. In view of the new turn of events, Belle saddled her horse and left it tied ready for an immediate departure. Then she settled down to rest. She did not sleep and heard the sound of approaching hooves. Rising, she went to the horses and stood by their heads. The riders were traveling along the trail at the top of the slope and could not see her. With any luck, they ought to pass without becoming aware of her presence.

Blowing down the slope, the wind carried the scent of its kind to the packhorse. Just a moment too late Belle lunged forward and caught the horse's nose to silence the whinny it gave. Seeing the riders turn and three of their number start in her direction, she knew there was only one thing to do. Releasing the packhorse, she freed her mount, swung into the saddle, and charged from the bushes. At first she thought of launching the canoe across the river, then decided to try to draw away the

Mexicans. Before she could turn the horse, a bullet ripped into it and it fell. Pitched from the saddle, Belle was winded by the fall and unable to resist when the men came down. With her Dance gone, she sat on the ground and studied her captors.

Only with an effort did Belle prevent her surprise showing at the sight of Eve Coniston riding with the Mexicans. At first Belle thought that she had fallen into Kraus's hands. On second thought, she concluded that the Yankee woman was also a prisoner. The poor-quality horse and bare feet did not suggest she, Eve, rode of her own free will.

After reaching this conclusion, Belle gave thought to her own predicament. Whatever happened, she must not let the others suspect her identity. If possible, she wanted to get them away from the area before any of them started nosing around and found the canoe.

"You wait till Bully hears what you done!" she screeched in the accent of a poor southerner. "He'll be riled about you-all shootin' my hoss!"

"Who are you, *señorita?*" Sandos asked.

"Rosie May Benstable, that's who!" Belle replied, conscious of Eve's eyes on her. "And I'm Bully Segan's best gal."

"She's got good boots, Joaquim," Juanita put in. "Nearly as good as mine."

"I want them!" Rosa yelled, drawing the knife from her belt and starting toward Belle.

Tensing slightly, Belle prepared to defend herself. She watched the men's faces and decided against making the attempt. Still partially winded by the fall, she could not give of her best. While a *savate* attack might, probably would, take Rosa by surprise, using it was not the answer. To demonstrate her skill would arouse the Mexicans' suspicions. Even if they failed to understand the significance of what they saw, the Yankee woman might. Already "Emily Corstin" had proved to be a smart, capable adversary and could be relied upon to draw the right conclusions. So Belle decided to avoid drawing too much attention to herself. Tangling in a hair-yanking brawl offered no way out, either. Rosa looked strong enough to make a hard fight. The longer they remained on the sandbar, the greater chance of somebody seeing the boat.

"Hey!" yelped Belle, backing off on her rump with well-simulated fear. "You'll keep her off me, d'you hear!"

"She want your boots, *señorita,*" Sandos pointed out.

"Then she c'n have 'em!" Belle wailed, starting to ease the right boot off.

While doing so, she glanced at Eve Coniston and saw the other showing more interest in her surroundings than the Mexicans. Then their eyes met and a smile flickered momentarily on Eve's lips. No matter what the Mexicans believed, Belle felt that she was not fooling the Yankee girl.

"Get the boots on *pronto,* Rosa!" Sandos ordered in Spanish, throwing a look toward the river. "The boats might come back and we don't want to be caught down here."

"What do we do with this one?" another of the gang inquired, indicating Belle with his thumb.

"Take her with us," Sandos replied. "If she's Bully Segan's woman, we'd better keep her for him."

"What's she going to ride?"

"Get her up behind the other gringo."

Having spent some of her time during the ride from Matamoros in improving her knowledge of Spanish, with Ysabel acting as tutor, Belle could follow the conversation. However, she gave no sign of understanding what she heard. The time might come when her apparent lack of comprehension would pay off.

Escape would be impossible while seated behind Eve on the swaybacked horse, even if Belle could rely on the Yankee to cooperate, so she made no attempt. In his eagerness to leave the river's edge, Sandos pushed his party at a good pace. So they missed noticing the tracks made by Belle and the Ysabels on their arrival.

Swinging away from the Rio Grande, they took a southeasterly direction for something over a mile. At last Sandos directed his horse into the mouth of a draw. As they turned a bend in the wide valley, they came into sight of the *bandido* camp. The fact that only two adobe *jacales* and a pole corral stood before them led Belle to assume the place was not the gang's main headquarters. Probably it served as no more than a temporary hideout handy for the border. From the general lack of life around the place, no other members of the gang were using it. Which still left six men and two women from whom Belle must escape.

"Put the women in there!" Sandos ordered, pointing to the smaller of the *jacales.* "When we've fed, we'll go across the river, spread out, and find Cosme."

"All of us?" Juanita asked.

"You and Rosa stop here to help Ruis guard the gringos," Sandos replied, and scowled at the girl. "Keep away from them until we learn what Cosme wants to do."

"*Sí,* Joaquim," she answered. "Maybe then we have some fun with them."

"Maybe," Sandos grunted. "Lock them in the *jacale.*"

On entering the smaller building, Eve and Belle looked around them. From all appearances the building had been used before for a similar purpose. Since its construction the window had been closed to mere slits and the door made strong to resist being broken open. Trying to do so would make sufficient noise to alert their captors. Belle studied the building, trying to decide how they might escape.

"You thought fast back there," Eve remarked, cutting into the other girl's thoughts. "Trying to lead them off like that. Then giving the girl your boots. If we'd stayed around that sandbar much longer, somebody might have seen that canoe."

"I don't know what you-all gettin' at, for sure," Belle answered. "When Bully comes—"

"Drop it, Boyd. I know you now, even if I didn't at the hotel in Matamoros," Eve interrupted. "What's wrong, did the Ysabels desert you?"

Realizing that her bluff had failed, Belle shrugged. "No. I suppose you're a Yankee spy?"

"Yes."

"Say! You must be Eve Coniston. I've heard about you."

Despite herself, Eve could not hold down a beam of pleasure at the words. That the legendary Rebel Spy knew of her meant her work had not gone unnoticed. Usually when Eve announced her vocation, people asked if she was Pauline Cushman. However, she put aside her thoughts and turned her attention back to their present situation.

"I thought one of them might see the canoe," she said. "I did."

"Why didn't you tell them?"

"If I had, we might both be dead, or wishing we were. Where're the Ysabels? Can we expect any help from them?"

"They went to Nava and won't be back until late afternoon at the earliest."

"I don't think we've that much time," Eve remarked. "It looks like you and I work together—or die."

"Why are they holding you?" Belle asked.

"For ransom," Eve explained. "My loyal companion told them what an important person I am."

Watching the bitter twist that came to Eve's lips, Belle could see how she felt and guess at its cause. When word of Eve's capture leaked out, the men who opposed using women for such important work would have another argument in their favor. Remembering the opposition to her own participation, Belle sympathized with Eve. She also realized that the other woman's feelings might make her more willing to cooperate in escaping.

"What happened to him?" Belle inquired.

"They shot him down in cold blood. Lord! I can't say I liked him as a man or a colleague, but even Ffauldes didn't deserve what he got."

"I don't know what you think," Belle remarked, "but I think we ought to try to escape."

"So do I," Eve stated grimly, showing Belle guessed correctly about her feelings. "The odds are steep against us doing it."

"Sandos is taking all but one man and the girls across the

river with him to look for their leader," Belle said. "If we don't escape before they get back with him, we'll never make it."

Before any more could be said, the door opened and the two Mexican girls entered, followed by Sandos. The man indicated the tin plates loaded with food that his companions carried.

"Eat well, *señoritas*," he ordered. "Cosme Danvila always feeds his visitors good—until he finds that nobody wants to pay to get them back."

Taking the plate, Belle almost held her breath as she waited to see what would happen next. Without even waiting for his prisoners to start eating, Sandos walked out of the cabin. Juanita limped a little as she followed the man and Rosa did not look any too happy in the unaccustomed footwear. As the lock clicked on the door, Belle looked at the plate. Then she smiled at Eve.

"I've an idea," she said. "Let's eat and I'll tell you about it."

For all the urgency of the business, Sandos and his men took their *siesta* before leaving to search for Danvila. Standing at the window slit in the front of the building, Belle watched the five men take their horses and ride away from the camp. She saw that four horses remained tied to the corral rails, but the man sat on the porch of the other *jacale* where he could see the animals and the front of the prisoners' quarters.

"We can't get to the horses with him there," Eve said, after taking a look.

"He'll have to be settled then," Belle answered. "The girls are still in the other cabin. If they don't come out before we're ready, it'll help us."

"Let's get started; they might remember the plates if we don't," Eve said.

Crossing to the rear wall, the two girls began to dig at the newer adobe of the window slit. At first they made no impression, then pieces began to crumble away with increasing regularity. Once started, the work progressed so well that one of them kept watch on the Mexican guard while the other continued digging.

"That'll do," Belle said at last, stepping back and studying the hole. "We don't want it too big or he might wonder why you didn't get through after me."

"He's still out front," Eve replied. "No sign of the girls."

Changing places, Eve went to stand by the enlarged rear window. She looked across at Belle, who halted between the door and the slit in the front wall. Then Eve turned and thrust her head through the hole.

"You stinking peckerwood* bitch!" the Yankee girl screeched at the top of her voice. "Come back here and help me!"

While the Mexican probably did not understand English, Eve declined to rely on it and so shouted the words she might have used at finding that her companion had deserted her.

"Ag—!" Belle began, then saw the man leap to his feet and run toward the building. He jerked a revolver Belle recognized as her Dance from his belt as he approached the door. "He's coming. Get ready!"

Twisting away from the lookout slit, Belle flattened her back against the wall on the hinged side of the door. Tense and alert, she listened to the lock click and watched the door open. Leaping in, his revolver held ready, the man glared at Eve as she turned from the rear wall. His eyes went to the hole and he drew just the conclusions they hoped he would. Clearly the two prisoners had attempted to escape, but the slim one had wriggled through the hole before making it large enough for her companion. Knowing how he would act under the circumstances, the man saw nothing out of the ordinary in Eve's behavior.

Letting out a snarl, the man advanced across the room. Again he acted just as Belle had hoped and placed himself in an ideal position for what she planned to do. Thrusting herself from the wall, she followed the man. The loss of her boots ruled out the use of several effective *savate* attacks, but she knew one that suited the conditions. Bounding into the air, she drew both feet up under her. At the full height of the leap, she straightened her legs and drove them at the man's back. With all the

---

* Peckerwood: derogatory name for a white southerner.

force she could manage, she crashed the bottom of her feet into the center of the man's back. Taken by surprise, he went reeling across the room. Eve sprang to meet him, sidestepping and sticking her right leg between his feet to trip him. Pitching headfirst into the wall, the man bounced away, landed on his back, and lay still.

Rebounding from the man after delivering her frontal leaping high kick, Belle started toward him. She saw that Eve needed no help and turned to face the door. Through it charged Rosa, a pistol in her hand. The girl no longer wore her looted boots and so made better time than Juanita, who clung to the footwear and was hobbling painfully across from the other *jacale*.

On arrival Rosa found herself faced with a tricky problem. The pistol she held was a muzzle-loading single-shot, and two potentially dangerous targets confronted her. While she vacilated between the gringos, Belle took the problem out of her hands. Even as Eve flung herself past the unconscious man, Belle darted forward. Once again the slim girl leapt into the air, but not in a kick. Passing over the pistol, she wrapped her legs about Rosa's neck. Breaking her fall with her hands, Belle let her shoulders hit the floor, then she twisted her body, pulling and using her weight to flip the Mexican over. A wail broke from Rosa as her feet left the floor, then she crashed down onto her back.

Beaten to Rosa by Belle, Eve still found work to do. Juanita entered the cabin walking awkwardly, which did not increase her efficiency. Springing past Belle, Eve slapped aside the revolver Juanita held. Then her other hand, knotted into a fist, drove hard into the Mexican girl's sizable bust. Giving a croaking cry, Juanita loosened her hold on the revolver. Eve slammed the trapped hand against the wall, completing the work of making Juanita release the weapon.

Turning her head, Eve saw Belle starting to rise and remembered about the canoe. The time for cooperation had ended and they became enemies once more. Catching the gasping Juanita by the hair, Eve hurled her at Belle. Just too late the southern girl realized Eve's intention. Juanita crashed into her and they went down in a heap. Swinging around, Eve darted through the door and slammed it behind her. For a moment she hesitated, hand halfway to the lock. Then she swung away without touching it. Maybe the Rebel Spy was an enemy, but Eve could not leave her trapped at the mercy of the *bandidos*. So she turned and ran to the waiting horses. Unfastening the reins of the best animal, she mounted. The stirrup irons hurt her feet, but she ignored the pain and started the horse moving.

With a heave Belle rolled Juanita from her and started to rise. Squealing curses, the other girl clawed at her and caught hold of her waistband. Cold rage filled Belle as she saw Eve's departure. The Yankee girl was not fleeing in blind panic. She knew where to find the canoe and could possibly make her escape along the Rio Grande in it.

"Like hell she will!" Belle gritted.

Despite the weight of the Mexican girl clinging to her, Belle got to her feet. Then she dug both hands into the black mass of hair and began to pull at it. Across the room, Rosa started to stir, moaning and writhing. Pain caused Juanita to draw away from Belle, although she still retained her hold. Up rammed Belle's left knee, driving into the Mexican girl's left breast. Twice more Belle sent her knee home before agony made the other release the hold on her belt. With a surging heave Belle threw Juanita from her. Going backward, the Mexican girl landed on her companion just as Rosa sat up. Pain made the girls oblivious of each other's identity. Hands dug into hair and they began to fight instead of rising to deal with Belle.

Running to the door, Belle tugged at it. Much to her surprise, she found it was not locked. However, by that time Eve had mounted and was already galloping along the draw. Anger made Belle act rashly for once. Instead of returning to the cabin and collecting her Dance, she dashed across to the waiting horses. Unfastening one of them, she swung into the saddle and set off after the fleeing Yankee spy.

14

A:HE, I CLAIM IT!

Sitting their horses in cover, the Ysabel Kid and his father studied the fort at Nava. As Sam Ysabel had told the Rebel Spy, the walls, designed to stand off an attack by arrows and rifle bullets, fared badly when assailed by cannon fire. However, the defenders were still holding out and there did not appear to be any chance of a rapid end to the siege.

"Can't see anybody we know well enough to trust, boy," Ysabel remarked.

"Nope," the Kid replied. "But there're a few there we know well enough *not* to trust. Damned if that's not old Marcus back there, all fancied up like a regular army officer."

"He was allus ambitious," Ysabel said. "If Benito Juarez does chase the French out, he'll have to watch his back against Marcus."

"Somebody'll chill Marcus's milk if he gets feisty," drawled the Kid.

Little did the Kid know, but he was fated to play a prominent part in the chilling process.*

"We'd best not get down there," Ysabel went on. "Marcus'd shoot us first and ask what we wanted while they buried us. Anyways, I don't feel right about leaving Miss Belle back by the river."

"Or me. What'll she do, *ap'*?"

"Damned if I know. Even if the Juaristas don't take the fort, I can't see Klatwitter having enough men or ammunition left to make their raid on New Mexico."

Turning their horses, they started the return journey. Indian-wise, they knew better than return along the route they had followed to Nava. Should somebody, French, Mexican or Kraus's gang, have come on their tracks, the Ysabels did not intend to simplify matters by going back along them. By riding relay, they had covered the distance to Nava in fast time and intended to return in the same manner. Three miles fell behind them. Then the Kid reined in his white stallion and pointed ahead.

"No Juaristas'd make that much smoke," he said.

"Nor Charlie Kraus, especially this close to Cosme Danvila's balliwick," Ysabel went on, studying the column of smoke that climbed upward from beyond a rim half a mile ahead. "They'll be French soldiers, I'd say."

Father and son exchanged glances. Several Mexican friends of long standing fought for Juarez, but the Ysabels had their duty to the Confederacy. So they must see if there was any way that relief could be brought to Klatwitter, even though doing so hurt the Juaristas' cause.

"We'd best go tell 'em what's happening at Nava," the Kid finally said.

"It's the only way," his father agreed.

Attacking unexpectedly, even a moderate-numbered French force might drive off the Juaristas. If the siege could be raised,

* Told in *The Peacemakers*.

Belle Boyd might yet visit Klatwitter and decide whether to continue with the plan.

As they rode on, the Ysabels watched the smoke. Although they had only just come into a position from which they could see it, both realized that it must have been visible for some time in other directions.

"Those frog soldiers sure must be lucky," the Kid remarked as they drew closer to the rim, "happen they allus make fires that smoke that ways."

"Likely there's no Injuns where they come from," his father replied. "Although a Creole feller I knowed one time allowed they had Apaches in Paris, France."

"I thought all the Apaches was over to New Mexico 'n' Arizona, 'cept for the Lipans in West Texas," the Kid said. "Happen them French Apaches're like our'n, I don't see how whoever's makin' that smoke's not wound up with their ears hangin' on some buck's lodge pole."

Topping the rim, they looked down and marveled still more. Eight French troopers and a sergeant were gathered around a fire, their carbines piled out of reach. Standing aloof at one side of the men, a young lieutenant was smoking a cigar. While four sentries covered the main points of the compass, each held his carbine on the crook of his arm and was doing his work inefficiently. Not one kept truly alert and each was looking in the wrong places. Such lack of caution might easily spell disaster. Discounting an Indian attack, the Juaristas claimed enough wild-country brains to read the signs and take appropriate action from what they learned.

Not until the Ysabels started to ride down the slope did any of the French soldiers notice them. Then the sentry nearest to them jerked his head around, brought his carbine to the ready position, and gave a yell. Belated though the warning might be, the soldiers moved with some speed. Dropping coffee cups, the troopers leapt toward their carbines. The officer spat away his cigar and swung to look at the newcomers. Discovering that they were not Mexicans, he barked an order that halted his men before they reached and unpiled the weapons.

Following the dictates of frontier etiquette, Ysabel halted his horse at the edge of the camp. He raised his hand in a peace sign and called, "Howdy. Mind if we'ns come up to the fire?"

"You may come," the officer answered in good English.

Swinging from their saddles and leaving the horses standing with trailing reins, the Ysabels walked forward. Studying the Frenchmen, Sam Ysabel liked little of what he saw. Tall, slim, handsome, the lieutenant's face held a hint of calculated cruelty. Ysabel summed him up as the kind of officer found all too frequently in the French army, a harsh disciplinarian who drove but never led men. Nor did the sergeant strike Ysabel in any more favorable a manner. Big, burly, brutal in appearance, he would blindly back up any order his officer gave.

"You gents headed for Nava?" Ysabel asked, noticing the envious manner with which the officer and sergeant were eyeing the four horses.

"Perhaps," the officer replied coldly.

"Happen you do," the big Texan drawled, "ride real careful. The Juaristas are attacking the fort down there."

"They attack the fort at Nava?" the officer repeated.

"Foot, hoss, and artillery," Ysabel confirmed. "Happen there's more of you around, I'd get 'em *pronto*. They're being bad hit at Nava and could use some help."

"Did Colonel Klatwitter send you?"

"He don't even know we're alive."

"Then how do you know of the attack?"

"We was down that ways and saw it."

"And what took you to Nava?" the lieutenant demanded.

"Me 'n' the boy know some folks down there and went visiting. Only when we saw the fighting, we concluded to head back across the river to home."

"Then why did you come to tell me of the attack?"

"You French folks've allus played square with the Confederacy," Ysabel replied. "So we allowed to come and give you the word."

All the time his superior and Ysabel were talking the French sergeant stood to one side studying first the Texans then their horses. Stepping forward, he saluted and spoke quietly to the officer in French. Nodding, the lieutenant replied and then turned back to Ysabel.

"Was the friend you intended to visit General Klatwitter?" he asked.

"Trouble, boy!" Ysabel grunted in Comanche to the Kid, although he never took his eyes from the officer's face or allowed a flicker of expression to show. "Plain folks like us don't get to make friends with generals, mister. So I don't know what you're meanin'."

"You don't?" the officer purred.

"Nary a notion," Ysabel answered.

"We have heard that two men and a girl take money to seduce General Klatwitter from his duty to France," the lieutenant explained. "Sergeant Manguer says he believes you are they."

"Don't see no gal along of us, do you, mister?" Ysabel drawled.

"Happen there is one around, you just tell me where to find her," the Kid went on with a grin. "I ain't seed a white gal in a coon's age."

Although he stood in what resembled a relaxed slouch, the youngster was tense with coiled-spring readiness. Like his father, he realized that coming to the French had been a serious error in tactics. Leaving again might prove even more difficult. Before coming to speak with his officer, the sergeant had flashed a signal to the troopers. Already the four sentries were lining their carbines at the Texans and the other men continued their interrupted gathering of piled carbines.

Used to the servile deference given by French enlisted men and Mexican peons, the officer found the Ysabels' attitude infuriatingly overfamiliar.

"Don't play games with me!" he blazed. "Not a few of those Juarista pigs have learned that Lieutenant Henri du Plessis is no man to trifle with."

"Mister," Ysabel drawled, "we come here to do you a service. Happen you don't want it, we'll be on our way."

"Not so fast!" du Plessis barked. "I am dissatisfied with your answers and intend to hold you for further questioning. Drop your gunbelts."

While on patrol along the Rio Grande, du Plessis had seen and challenged the three Yankee steam launches. He had learned of the Rebel Spy's mission and had changed his route in the hope of finding her before she reached Klatwitter. Avarice showed on his face as he studied the Texans and wondered if Manguer had guessed correctly. They did not have a woman along, nor carry saddle pouches bulky enough to hold the large sum of money mentioned by the men from the launches. So he wanted to take them alive if possible and see if they would give useful information under questioning.

Even if they should not be the men seeking Klatwitter, killing them would produce some valuable loot. Four good, if hard-run, horses, a Sharps rifle, and two Dragoon Colts—so much more effective than the Le Mat and Lefauchex revolvers issued by the French army—could not be picked up every day of the week. Nor was there likely to be any comeback over the killings. The Confederate States government could hardly complain at the death of two agents while on a mission to seduce an entire French regiment from its duty. And if the men were not Confederate agents it seemed unlikely that such unimportant people would be missed.

"Damned if we don't oughta make him kill us, so's he'll try to ride ole Nigger there," the Kid remarked to his father, having read du Plessis's feelings toward the white stallion in the avaricious study of it. "Do you see 'em, *ap*'?"

"Just now did. Likely there're waiting to see how things go," Ysabel answered and turned his attention to du Plessis. Much as he disliked the Frenchman, he felt that he must give a warning. "Soldier boy, was I you, I'd tell your fellers to set them carbines down, go get their hosses, and be ready to ride for Nava."

"You tell me nothing!" du Plessis yelled, wild with fury at the lack of deference showed by the Ysabels. "I will count to three, by which time you will drop your gunbelts and surrender." Then in French he told Manguer of his intentions and added, "Shoot them in the legs when I say 'two'."

"Oui, mon lieutenant," Manguer replied, realizing the importance of taking the Texans alive.

Drawing his revolver, the sergeant began to raise it and du Plessis commenced his treacherous count.

"One!"

Something swished through the air, flying from the slope opposite to that down which the Ysabels had come to the camp. Even as his finger squeezed at the trigger ready to carry out his orders, Manguer's back arched in sudden pain. Shock and agony twisted his face as he took an involuntary pace forward. Dropping the revolver, he clawed at the head of an arrow that burst through the left breast of his tunic. Vainly trying to draw the arrow from him, he sank to his knees, collapsed face forward, and spasmodically kicked as his lifeblood soaked into the Mexican soil.

Attracted by the same smoke that had led the Ysabels to the French, the band of *Pahuraix* raiders reached the scene shortly after the Texans arrived. Seeing the two men who claimed such close ties with Long Walker of the *Pehnane,* the chief did not launch an immediate attack. However, it soon became obvious that the Texans were not among friends and the braves moved forward. Neglecting their duty, all the sentries were watching what happened to their visitors and failed to see the deadly advance. Witnessing the sergeant aiming his revolver at Ysabel, the chief took a hand. The short Comanche bow, designed for use on the back of a fast-running horse, packed enough power to sink a thirty-six-inch arrow flight deep into the muscular back of a bull buffalo. It proved no less successful when used against a human being.

Showing commendable restraint, the rest of the party let their chief commence the attack. However, all held their weapons ready and turned loose a volley as their leader's bowstring vibrated. Arrows, and bullets from the few rifles in the group, tore down into the unsuspecting Frenchmen.

Four troopers and the sergeant died in that first deadly as-

sault, but the rest did not panic and prepared to fight. Nor did
the arrival of the Indians cause the French to forget their original visitors.

Throwing up his carbine, a trooper snapped a shot that sent
Ysabel's hat spinning from his head. On the heels of the shot,
the big Texan drew and fired his Dragoon. Ysabel shot to kill,
not only to prevent another attempt on himself but to make
sure the soldier did not fall alive into the hands of the
Pahuraix.

No Comanche worth his salt would be content to stand back
from an enemy. A coup counted by bullet or arrow rated lower
than one gained in personal contact. So after the first volley,
they charged recklessly forward at the remains of the French
party.

Out flashed du Plessis's saber and he flashed a quick glance
around. Quick maybe, but it told him all he needed to know.
Nothing could save his men, and he saw no reason to die with
them. Not when the means of escape lay so near. Not his own
horse, for that stood picketed with his men's close to where the
Indians attacked. However, four fine mounts were waiting for
him in a position that offered a clear run to safety. Mounted on
that magnificent white stallion, he could escape while the remains of his command fought to their deaths.

With that thought in mind, he sprang in the direction of the
horses. Before he took three strides, he found his way blocked
by an obstacle that must be removed if he hoped to carry on. At
first he did not recognize the obstacle. Although still dressed in
his white man's clothing, the Ysabel Kid's face looked no less
savage than those of the attacking Comanches. Steel glinted in
the Kid's hand also, but for once the bowie knife looked almost
dwarfed alongside its opposite number.

During his career in the army, du Plessis had fought in several duels and not all of the *au premier sang*—which ended
when blood, no matter how slight, was drawn—variety pre-
scribed in regulations. A fine swordsman, he expected no trouble in dealing with the tall youngster. What he failed to take
into consideration was that he faced a *man* trained from early

childhood in all the rudiments and refinements of fighting with
cold steel, yet whose schooling did not conform to the accepted
precepts of the continental *code duello.*

Going into the attack, du Plessis launched a cut at the Kid's
head and confidently expected to batter down the other's guard
to reach his target. However, the youngster knew better than to
try to parry a saber blow with even a James Black bowie knife.
Instead he seemed to go two ways at the same moment. From
landing on the ground in a forward step, the right foot thrust
backward and the Kid moved to the rear, outside the saber's
lethal arc.

Taken by surprise at the failure of his attack, du Plessis still
caught his balance and returned the saber with a sweeping inside swing to the head. Again he missed, for the Kid thrust,
cut, and lunged at the illusive shape before him. Oblivious to
the fight that was raging behind them, the Kid and du Plessis
fought their strange duel. While the Kid's long knife never met
the saber, neither did the *arme blanche* make hit on him.

Leaping over a low cut, the Kid landed inside the blade and
his knife ripped across. For the first time du Plessis found need
to show his own agility. He tried to avoid the Kid's attack by a
hurried spring to the rear. Slicing through the French tunic, the
tip of the bowie knife carved a shallow gash across its wearer's
chest. Pain stung du Plessis, although he knew the wound to be
superficial. However, he realized that he must bring the fight to
a speedy end and kill that deadly savage who stood between
him and the horses. Doing it with the saber would consume too
much time.

Again he sprang to the rear, and the Kid started after him.
Whipping back his arm, du Plessis hurled his saber at the Kid.
Then the officer sent his right hand flashing toward the revolver
at his belt. Shining brightly and looking militarily smart, the
holster did not lend itself to a fast draw.

Like a giant dart, the saber hurled at the Kid, but he went
under it in a rolling dive that wound up with him in a kneeling
position almost at du Plessis's feet. Up drove the Kid's blade,
its point gouging into the Frenchman's belly—always the knife-

fighter's favorite target. With a croaking cry of pain du Plessis stumbled backward and began to double over. Again the Kid struck, almost in a continuation of the move that tore the knife free from its first mark. Coming upward and back, the curved false edge, as sharp as the blade itself, sank into flesh. It sliced through the windpipe, veins, and arteries of the throat almost to the bone. Gagging in an effort to breathe, blood spouting from the terrible gash, du Plessis went down.

"*A:he,* I claim it!" breathed the Kid.

Behind him a French trooper turned a Le Mat revolver in his direction. Coming up from behind, the *Pahuraix* war chief swung his fighting ax to sever the soldier's spine and drop him instantly to the ground. Springing past his chief, a young brave sank his knife into the dying trooper and claimed the coup.

Then it was all over. Standing with his smoking Dragoon in hand, Ysabel looked around him. With something like relief he saw that none of the soldiers had been taken alive. If any had fallen into the Comanches' hands, there was little enough Ysabel could have done to save them. Nor could he interfere in any way with the aftermath of the victory.

"My thanks, *Soldado Pronto,*" the Kid said, wiping clean his knife on du Plessis's tunic. "The smoke brought you here?"

"Yes," the chief replied. "This has been a poor raid, Cuchilo. Everywhere we found soldiers and little loot."

"You have horses, guns, and bullets here," Ysabel pointed out, joining his son. Then he pointed unerringly toward Nava. "Down that way is a big fight; many soldiers are going there."

"I think we go and see what we can take," the chief stated.

"And we must ride to meet my squaw," Ysabel answered.

"It's lucky we come back," the Kid said as he and his father rode away and the *Pahuraix* braves set about the business of gathering loot. "They were headed for the border and might've found Miss Belle."

"Yep!" Ysabel agreed. "And with their medicine looking so bad, they might've took their meanness out on her."

Riding on, they swung somewhat to the east of their original line and came into sight of the two *jacales* from which Belle

and Eve had escaped. They brought their horses to a halt, ears
catching certain significant sounds. Mingled with a scuffling
sound and screams from the smaller building was the drumming of rapidly departing hooves. At first they saw no sign of
life, other than the horses at the corral. Then the two exhausted
but still fighting Mexican girls reeled through the front door
and sprawled to the ground.

"What the hell?" Ysabel exclaimed, starting his horses moving. "This's one of Danvila's hideouts, but there don't look to
be any of his fellers around."

If there had been any of the gang present, it was unlikely
they would miss such a prime piece of excitement as what
looked to have been one hell of a good girl fight.

"Wonder who it was rode off," the Kid went on. "Two of
'em. Way the hooves sounded, I'd say one following the other
and both going like the devil after a yearling."

"Best go take a look and pull them two apart afore they
snatch each other baldheaded," Ysabel suggested.

Before the men reached them, the girls rose to their knees
and pitched back into the *jacale*. Alert for a trap, Ysabel and
the Kid dismounted, drew their Colts, and followed the girls.
Looking over the fighting pair, the Kid studied the man lying
by the rear wall. Then he glanced at the hole and dropped his
eyes to the revolver at the man's side.

Forgetting the girls, the Kid darted across and picked up the
revolver. At first glance it looked like a well-made Navy Colt.
Only the Kid knew different. The revolver bore the unmistak-
able signs of being made by the Dance brothers of Columbia,
Texas. More than that, its ivory handle and superior finish
proved it to be the gun they made for and presented to the
Rebel Spy as a tribute to her good work.

"Miss Belle'd never part with this unless there was no way
she could help it!" the Kid growled. "They must've got her."

"And she's got away again," his father went on. "Likely that
was her runnin' with one of 'em after her we heard."

"Let's get goin' after her and see!" the Kid barked, thrusting
the Dance into his belt and running toward the door.

Although the Ysabels wasted no time in mounting, when they reached the end of the draw they could see no sign of whoever had fled before their arrival. So they pushed on in the direction of the sandbar. With tired horses under them, they could not make as fast a pace as they wished. However, they rode on, hoping for a sight of the people they were following. Suddenly they heard shooting ahead. Not just rifles and carbines, but the crack of a light cannon and a harsh staccato rattle that reminded Ysabel of the sound made by an Ager Coffee-Mill machine gun.

Jerking their rifles from the medicine boots, Sam Ysabel and the Kid urged their leg-weary mounts on toward the head of the slope that hid the river—and the sandbar where they had left the money in the canoe—from view.

15

TAKE HER OUT COMANCHE FASHION

By the time Belle Boyd had selected, freed, and mounted the best of the remaining horses, Eve Coniston had built up a good lead in the race for the canoe. While a good horsewoman, Eve could not equal Belle's skill. However, no amount of ability could offset the superior mount Eve sat, and Belle failed to close the distance no matter how she urged on her horse.

Wondering if the Rebel Spy had managed to make good her escape, Eve fought down a desire to look back. She wished to avoid anything that might jeopardize her chances. To take her attention off the horse and where she rode might cause a fall. As she rode, she decided on her course of action. At the sandbar she would shove off and board the canoe, then either paddle down the river or allow the current to take her. Either way, the steam launches would find her. Then she could continue down to Brownsville at all speed and deliver the money to the authorities. With it as evidence, the United States government ought to be able to demand that Great Britain prevent any recurrence of the attempt.

On Eve rode, keeping the horse at a gallop. At last she saw the sandbar, identifying it for certain by the dead horse lying by the water's edge. Down the slope she went, almost losing her balance. At the foot, she jumped from the saddle and let the horse go free. If all went well she would not need it again, and she could not spare valuable seconds to secure it.

Even as Eve reached the canoe and tugged at its fastenings, she heard the drumming of hooves. Turning her head, she saw Belle Boyd galloping into sight. She swung back to the canoe, jerking the knot open and throwing the rope aside. Then she began to haul the canoe out from under its covering, turning its bows toward the center of the river as soon as she could.

A glance over her shoulder told Eve how little time she had. Riding with reckless abandon, Belle plunged down the incline. The slim southern girl left the saddle as the horse reached the foot of the slope and ran across the sand. Belle knew she would be too late to prevent the launching of the canoe, but figured she could still destroy its load. Although she had no means of igniting the powder charges, she felt that upturning the canoe and dumping them into the river would suffice. Under the surface lay quicksand, according to the Kid. Once the kegs reached them, recovery would be impossible.

Realizing that she could not hope to board the canoe and escape, Eve did not try. Instead she gave it a hard push and watched it carried forward across the water. Then she swung around to face Belle. What a triumph it would be if she could deliver the Rebel Spy along with the gold to Brownsville. The smug male crowd who insisted that women had no place in the Secret Service would be hard pressed to find an argument to that achievement.

However, Eve knew capturing Belle Boyd would be anything but easy. From what she had seen at the *jacale,* and suspected had happened to the French sergeant in Matamoros, the southern girl could handle her end of any rough stuff that came along. So could Eve if it came to that.

During the ride to the *jacales,* being seated behind Eve and holding on to her waist had allowed Belle to form an estimate of the other's physical condition. So Belle had an idea of Eve's strength. Yet the older woman showed no sign of knowing other than female ways of defending herself. Charging forward with hands raised and fingers hooked like talons, Eve seemed to be wide open for a *savate* attack. Barefooted or not, Belle felt sure a stamping side kick would take most of the aggression out of the older woman.

So Belle skidded to a halt, going into a *savate* fighting stance and swinging herself into position to deliver the kick. As her leg rose, she saw a change come over Eve. Down came the woman's hands, thumbs touching and with the fingers forming a U shape into which Belle's ankle slipped to be halted. Clamping hold of the ankle, Eve swung the leg around and twisted the foot. Belle felt her other foot leave the ground, then she went somersaulting over. Long training at riding helped her to break her fall on the soft sand.

Springing after Belle, Eve raised her right leg and stamped. Her heel drove into Belle's side as the girl rolled over, instead of striking her stomach. While painful, the stamp did not slow Belle down as it would if it had landed on its intended mark. So she was ready when Eve followed her and tried to repeat the stamp. Twisting herself over in Eve's direction, Belle caught the ankle on which she stood in one hand and placed the other on the knee. By tugging forward at the ankle and shoving back on the knee, she overbalanced the older woman. Eve yelled as she fell on to her back on the sand.

Like a flash Belle hurled herself onto Eve, trying to pin down her arms as a prelude to driving home punches at the other's face and torso. Belle knew Eve was strong, and learned the extent of her strength. Heaving herself upward, until only the soles of her feet and top of her head rested on the sand, Eve pitched the lighter girl off her. Rolling on top, Eve locked her fingers about Belle's throat and began to squeeze. Desperately Belle heaved and shook to try to tip the other woman from her. Eve's fingers clamped home hard, tightening savagely, and

Belle knew she must escape the grip. Fighting down the near panic which caused her to waste energy striking wildly at Eve's face, Belle reached up and clutched at the front of the mauve blouse. Pain knifed into Eve as Belle's fingers dug into and crushed at her bust. Croaking curses, she tried to raise Belle's head and crash it down again. The effort proved only partially successful, for the soft sand cushioned the impact and Belle's neck muscles fought against it. Nor did the slim fingers relax their hold; they continued to dig into the sensitive mounds of flesh. Giving a screech of agony, Eve tried to rise without releasing her hold on Belle's throat. As Eve stood up, Belle curled both feet between her spread-apart legs, placed them against her midsection, and heaved. Losing her grip on Belle, Eve felt the fingers dragged from her bust. Then she flew over and landed on her back.

That first exchange gave Belle a grim warning. Eve possessed strength at least equal to and probably greater than her own. Tangling at close quarters would be dangerous. So she rolled over to a kneeling position and rose. Sucking in deep breaths of air, she swung to face Eve, who had also made it to her feet. For a moment the older woman stood rubbing at her bust, then she clenched her fists and advanced. No longer did she act like an untrained woman, but came forward in the manner of a trained male pugilist. Belle moved to meet Eve in much the same manner, except that she favored the stance of the *savate* fighter.

When they came together, it might have been two men fighting. Their fists flew, smacking hard into face, bust, stomach as they circled. Any slight advantage Belle might have gained by her speed was countered by Eve's small strength superiority. Blood ran from Eve's nose and Belle's lip, their breath came in gasping hisses, but they fought on, oblivious to everything except each other. Bony knuckles smacked solidly against Eve's already throbbing nose. She stumbled back a couple of paces, screamed, and flung herself at the advancing Belle. Swept backward by the older woman's weight, Belle collided with the dead horse. Still locked together, the women fell over it, landing on the sand to churn over and over in a wild tangle. They went at it completely oblivious to everything but each other, and neither saw the two riders who came into view on the slope across the river.

"Madre de dios!" Sandos spat out as he saw the two women rolling over and over by the dead horse. Even at that distance he could recognize them. "It's the gringos I told you about, Cosme. How the hell did they escape?"

Middle-sized, stocky, and hard-looking despite his elegant clothing, Cosme Danvila let out a low growl. "We'll find out whe—Hey! Look at that canoe."

Carried forward by its light weight and Eve's shove, the canoe had reached the center of the river. The sluggish current at that point turned the canoe's bows downstream and floated it along slowly. Pleased that something had taken his leader's thoughts off how the prisoners escaped, Sandos decided to try to keep them that way.

"Maybe that other one isn't Bully Segan's woman," he said hurriedly. "She could be the one who was with Big Sam Ysabel, taking the gold to the French general at Nava."

"I never knew Bully to have a woman who wasn't fat as a pig and ugly," Danvila answered. "You told me the old one was a spy for the United States, and the other will work for the Confederacy. Get the men—that canoe has the money in it!"

While Sandos turned to obey, Danvila looked at the kegs in the canoe. He had guessed pretty accurately what had happened, from the Ysabels hiding the money until learning if the French general could be trusted, through Belle's actions at the time of her capture, to the women's escape—somebody was going to wish they had never been born allowing that to happen —and why they were fighting. One of them must have pushed it off, meaning to escape, and the other was trying to prevent her from doing so. On the latter point Danvila wasted no time or thought. Whatever had started the fight, he intended to have the money. A large sum in gold would be a godsend at a time when French and Juarista soldiers were making banditry unprofitable below the border and Captain Jack Cureton's hard-fighting Rangers rendered it extremely unsafe in Texas.

On the sandbar, unaware of the new threat to their existence, Eve expended much of her remaining dregs of energy heaving Belle away from her. The tangle on the ground had been rough, with teeth, fists, knees, elbows, and heads used indiscriminately. Their blouses hung in tatters, their underwear was torn, and Eve's skirt had split up its left side. Croaking in breaths of air, they both began to rise. Pain and exhaustion gnawed at Eve, for Belle's youth and superb physical condition had combined to wear the older woman down. Eve stumbled back, away from Belle, hoping to gain a respite during which she could gather her flagging strength for a further effort. Sensing the other's condition, Belle clenched her fists and advanced. If she could continue the attack quickly enough, Eve was beaten.

Leading his men down the slope, Danvila saw the three steam launches come into sight around the river's upstream bend. With almost fifty well-armed men at his back, and the chance of laying hands on fifteen thousand dollars as an inducement, the *bandido* leader saw no reason to call off his attempt. Faced by a body of men on land, be they sheriff's posse, company of Texas Rangers, or members of the Mexican *Guardia Rurales,* he could have estimated the danger immediately. However, he knew nothing of naval power. While he recognized the cannon, the true potential of the Gatling gun in the leading launch escaped him. Like Amy-Jo, he took the six-barreled machine gun to be some strange form of cannon, single-shot and not especially dangerous. So he yelled to his men to kill the gringos, jerked out his revolver, and fired toward the river.

Seated forward on the gunwale of the launch commanded by the lieutenant, the Gatling's gunner saw the canoe. At his lookout's yell, the lieutenant moved toward the bows. Taking in the canoe and the sight of the two tattered, exhausted women getting to their feet on the sandbar, the officer guessed what might be happening. Even before Eve's assistant in the second launch, or Golly in his own, could speak, the lieutenant opened his mouth to give orders. He meant to tell the launch nearest to the Mexican shore to land and bring aboard the women. A bullet, flying down from the Texas bank of the river, struck his launch's funnel and chopped off the words unsaid.

More shots sounded and a sailor cried out, clutching at his bleeding chest as he toppled over the side of the third launch. That drew the crews' attention to the approaching Mexicans. Veterans of the Mississippi Squadron's river campaigns, the sailors knew how to deal with such an attack, whether it be delivered by Confederate cavalry or a rabble of Mexican border thieves.

Without needing orders the gunners sprang to their pieces and started twirling elevating screws to line the barrels upward. Their assistants leapt forward to throw open the ammunition lockers under the decking that supported the guns. Already the coxswains were thrusting on the tillers to point the launches' bows in the required direction, and the engineers cut off the propellers to prevent them from being run aground. Other members of the crews grabbed up Spencer carbines or drew their Navy Colts.

Before Danvila and his men fully realized the extent of their danger, the flotilla opened fire. With a sullen double roar, the two twelve-pounders vomited out their loads. Each cannon was charged with canister, the twenty-seven 1.5-inch balls turning it into a kind of enormous shotgun, deadly up to a range of three hundred and fifty yards. Their detonations mingled with the harsh chatter as the man behind the Gatling gun whirled its firing handle around, turning the barrels in their loading cycle to spurt flame and lead as each muzzle reached the uppermost point of its axis.

Caught in the blast of flying lead, the *bandido* gang suffered badly. Men and horses went down. Flung over its head by his mount's collapse, Danvila fell into the path of the Gatling gun's bullets. His body arched as three of them ripped into him, then went limp and rolled a few feet down the slope. Desperate hands hauled back on reins, trying to swing the horses away from the hail of death. Then the shattered remnants of Danvi-

la's gang plunged back up the slope. They left ten dead and
seven wounded behind in their flight. Not until the last of the
gang had passed out of sight over the rim could the lieutenant
spare a thought for the two women.

At the sound of the shooting Belle stopped in her tracks and
started to look around. She had her back to the river, so failed
to see the new arrivals. Exhausted she might be, but Eve saw
them and recognized that help was on hand. Taking a stagger-
ing step forward, she swung a roundhouse punch to the side of
Belle's jaw. Taken completely by surprise, Belle went down to
land spread-eagled on her back. Dazed by the blow, she lay
motionless. Breath whistling through her mouth, Eve stumbled
toward the slim girl. The woman intended to fall knees first on
to Belle's stomach and finish her off. Through the mists that
seemed to be swirling around in her head, Belle saw Eve's advance and guessed her intention. Yet the girl could not make
herself do anything to prevent the move.

Then an explosion split the air, its sound all but drowning
out the double crack of rifle fire that wafted down from the rim
on the Mexican shore. On the river, the canoe disappeared in a
sheet of flame and cloud of black smoke. Tossed up by the blast,
a sizable wave rushed on to the launches. Each boat had men
flung over the side by the unexpected pitching, and the one
closest to the explosion took a considerable amount of water
aboard as it rocked violently.

On the bank Eve staggered as the shock wave of air hit her
but she did not fall. The halt in Eve's advance gave Belle just
that brief moment she needed to recover. Coiling up her body,
Belle thrust her legs forward and up with all her remaining
strength. Reeling forward again, Eve took the soles of Belle's
driving feet full in the pit of her stomach. A strangled croak
broke from the Yankee as she doubled over, pitched backward,
and crashed helplessly to the sand. All but spent by her final
effort, Belle rolled onto her stomach. She could not force herself higher than to hands and knees. Yet she knew that she must
try to escape. Weakly, sobbing at the effort, she started to crawl
in the direction of the bushes.

At the top of the slope overlooking the sandbar, Sam Ysabel and the Kid watched the result of their shooting. When they came into view of the river, they had seen immediately what must be done. No bunch of Mexican *bandidos* ever born would face up to what Danvila and his men received from the launches. With the gang disposed of, the Yankees could easily catch up with the canoe. So there was only one course left open to the two Texans. Sighting their rifles, they planted a bullet each into the powder kegs. Some of the gold coins might land on the banks, but the vast majority of them sank irrecoverably into the quicksand at the bottom of the river. That left only one problem needing a hurried solution.

"We've got to rescue Miss Belle!" the Kid stated, coming to his feet.

"Yeah!" Ysabel replied. "We'll take her out Comanche fashion."

Running to their waiting horses, they thrust the rifles into the saddleboots, freed the spare mounts, and swung into the saddles. Side by side, the father and son headed over the rim and down toward the sandbar.

Occupied with the work of bailing out their launches and helping comrades back aboard, the Yankee sailors did not notice the Ysabels. Golly saw them first, guessed what they meant to do, and yelled a warning.

Painfully Belle dragged herself along the sand. Although she could hear the thunder of approaching hooves, the sound meant nothing to her. Directing their horses to pass on either side of the girl, the Ysabels leaned inwards and reached down. Belle felt a hand take hold of each arm and raise her, then carry her along. Shouts rang out as the Yankees realized a rescue bid was being made. Golly's revolver barked twice, but its bullets came nowhere near the fast-moving Texans. Other men grabbed at weapons, their excited movements threatening to capsize the boats.

"Belay that shooting!" roared the lieutenant. "Mr. Snaith, run your launch ashore and bring Miss Coniston off. She looks like she needs help."

With the bushes close ahead, there could be no more carrying Belle between them. So Ysabel reached across with his other hand, took hold, and swung the girl's limp body up before him. Supporting her in his arms, he used knee pressure to guide the grulla in among the undergrowth. Showing superb horsemanship, the Kid allowed his father to go first and plunged into cover after him. Letting Ysabel ride on, the Kid collected the packhorse and its saddles before following.

Not until they had put two miles between them and the river did the Texans stop. While the Kid made a fire and set up camp for the night, Ysabel helped Belle tend to her injuries. At last the girl lay on a bed of soft grass, her numerous bruises and aching muscles sending knifelike jagged stabs of pain through her. Yet she barely felt them in the sick, numbing realization that her mission had ended in failure. The Kid had brought along the packs that held her property and disguised weapons, but the gold on which so much depended lay at the bottom of the Rio Grande. Without it Klatwitter would not make a move, even if he could after the attack on the fort at Nava. Nothing the Ysabels could say offered her any comfort.

"I've failed!" she moaned. "Everything is lost."

Little did Belle know that the failure had probably been the most fortunate thing to happen to her.

The date was April the 8th, 1865. Next day at the Appomattox courthouse, wishing to prevent further bloodshed and loss of life, General Robert E. Lee surrendered his sword to General U.S. Grant as a preliminary to bringing the War Between the States to an end.

J.T. EDSON

Brings to Life the Fierce and Often Bloody Struggles of the Untamed West

___ THE BAD BUNCH	20764-9	$3.50
___ THE FASTEST GUN IN TEXAS	20818-1	$3.50
___ NO FINGER ON THE TRIGGER	20749-5	$3.50
___ SLIP GUN	20772-X	$3.50
___ TROUBLED RANGE	20773-8	$3.50
___ JUSTICE OF COMPANY Z	20858-0	$3.50
___ McGRAW'S INHERITANCE	20869-6	$3.50
___ RAPIDO CLINT	20868-8	$3.50
___ COMMANCHE	20930-7	$3.50
___ A MATTER OF HONOR	20936-6	$3.50
___ WACO RIDES IN	21019-4	$3.50

FLOATING OUTFIT SERIES

___ THE HIDE AND TALLOW MEN	20862-9	$3.50
___ THE NIGHTHAWK	20726-6	$3.50
___ RENEGADE	20964-1	$3.50